Chasing Nathan

Jeanette Hubbard

PROMONTORY
P R E S S

Chasing Nathan
Copyright 2015 by Jeanette Hubbard

Promontory Press
www.promontorypress.com

ISBN: 978-1-987857-43-6

Typeset by One Owl Creative in 13pt Bembo
Cover design by Marla Thompson of Edge of Water Design
Cannabis by Joey Sabey from the Noun Project

Printed in Canada
098765432

Chasing Nathan

Chapter One

Wednesday afternoon

Claudie gripped one end of the tent pole and eased it into the end thingy and then scooted around to the opposite side and strained to lift the nylon tent and steady it so she could insert the other pole end into the opposite end thingy. She almost had it when the first one sprang from its position and the tent flopped in a puddle of bright green nylon. Bloody hell. It was going to be a challenge to get this puppy up by herself. But she had put a lot of tents up in her day, and she wasn't going to be defeated by something a teenager could put up in ten minutes. It was really simple. Two long flexible fiberglass poles threaded through pole sleeves that crisscrossed on the roof of the tent and then bent and inserted into the end thingies (whatever they were called in REI speak), on each bottom corner of the tent and *voilà*, with a snap the tent stands. Easy peasy.

Ten minutes and six attempts later, she glared at the still supine tent. Damn, it wasn't rocket science. Peter had shown her how to put the tent up and it hadn't seemed to be all that hard. Not that much different from her old tent. Perhaps she hadn't paid enough attention. The problem was, without someone to hold onto one side, the flexible poles kept springing out of the end thingies. She almost had it once, but a light breeze puffed up the tent like a balloon and threw the balance off.

She was getting hot and her back was hurting. She went over to the car and dragged the ice chest out and pulled it over to the picnic table. It was time for a break and a glass of wine. She sat and looked at the collapsed tent and then around at the empty campground. The euphoria of finding such a beautiful campground along the Rogue River, which was completely bereft of RVs and other signs of campers, was dissipating in the realization that she might need help with the tent. She poured a glass of Oregon Pinot Gris and sat watching the sunlight filtering through the giant Ponderosa pines. After about fifteen minutes she heaved a sigh. The damn tent wasn't going to raise itself.

Once again, she bent the poles and this time she succeeded in getting three of the four poles in place. Cautiously she gripped the end of the fourth pole, the tent was precariously up and swaying in the light breeze. All she had to do was get this end hooked into its thingy and she … Bloody, bloody hell! Just as the end slipped into place, she heard a snap. She straightened up and could see a jagged pole edge pushing through the sleeve at the top of the tent. The tent was up, true, but it now had a drunken slant to it. It looked like a harsh word would send it collapsing to the ground. She walked over to the picnic table, poured another glass of the white wine, and sat staring at the treacherous tent. The light wind played with the green nylon, billowing it in and out like it was breathing. Traitorous beast. After quiet contemplation of her options, like going back to Grant's Pass and staying in some dismal motel, or somehow jury-rigging some way to keep the tent from collapsing, she chose the stay put option. Somewhere in her trunk there was some rope. And there was no shortage of trees.

Her head was buried in the trunk of the car when she heard a vehicle slowly drive into the campground. She stood and watched as a mini-motorhome crept down the gravel road. Sure, now someone shows up. The man driving the small RV gave her a brief wave and drove on. He circled the entire campground loop and then came around again, stopping in a space two down from Claudie's. Thankfully there were several shrubs and trees in between, so she was mostly screened off from her new neighbor. She resumed her search for the rope and found a fluorescent orange nylon rope at the bottom of her emergency travel box.

She studied the tree nearest her tent; it was an alder with a low branch arching over the green tent. Perfect. She played out some of the rope and then gave it a sturdy toss. It snaked out about two feet under the branch. She pulled it back, gave it a bit of a wind-up, and pitched it again. This time it hit the branch and, with a crack, the branch broke off and fell to the ground, missing the tent by about three feet. Hmmm. None of the other low branches were hanging near the tent. She looked at the tree, trying to think of other options. She heard a crunch of gravel behind her and turned to see a man standing on the road at the edge of her campsite. Christ. With a bit of chagrin she recognized him. It was Nathan. He owned the bookstore in Sisters and had asked her out for coffee twice. She had put him off both times.

"Claudie?"

"Hi, Nathan. Small world."

"It can appear that way at times. Are you having problems with your tent? Or are you just practicing your roping skills?" He smiled gently. He was really a nice looking man. In his early sixties, wavy grey hair on the longish side, blue eyes, a kind of Gary Cooper build that she liked on men. He was sporting a couple of days' growth of beard and he didn't look as buttoned down as usual. It was just that he was too nice. She wasn't good around nice men. When she was younger she had chewed them up and left them in a puddle of heartbreak so fast that it was dizzying. It wasn't a good idea now that she was living in a small town like Sisters to litter the area with hurt feelings. Of course she realized that now she had hit sixty-one there was considerably less likelihood that she could inflict much damage. Still, misunderstandings can happen at any age. And really, she was too old for the drama of romance.

"I apparently have no roping skills to speak of. One of the poles on the tent broke. I'm just trying to figure out a way to keep it from caving in on me in the middle of the night."

Nathan walked up to the tent and eyed the jagged edge poking through the nylon pole sleeve. He turned and started walking back to his RV. "I think I can fix this for you. Give me a sec."

Not too proud to be rescued, Claudie took her seat again at the picnic table and waited. In a few minutes he returned with a roll of duct tape. Damn, the old duct tape trick. Why hadn't she thought of that? He proceeded to pull the damaged pole out and wrap it with several layers of grey tape. Then, with Claudie's help, he threaded the pole again and they lifted the tent. Nathan easily slipped the end of the repaired pole into the end thingy and she had a tent that was now operational.

"I can't thank you enough. Could I offer you a glass of wine?" It was the least she could do after all.

He glanced at his watch, "I guess it's close enough to five. Sure."

"Red or white?" She pulled a wine tote that held six bottles of wine from the back of her car.

"Whoa. You're prepared. How long were you planning on camping?"

"About a week. I figured that if I ran out I could always run into town." Nathan's mouth twitched in a brief smile, "I prefer red."

Claudie opened a bottle of Cabernet Sauvignon and poured him a glass.

"Real wine glasses to boot. I see you camp in style, Claudie." He sat down on the end of the picnic table and stretched out his long legs.

"Why not? Besides, plastic ruins the taste of wine."

"This is a nice big Cab. From Walla Walla?" Claudie nodded and he continued, "I've always loved this campground. It's so peaceful. Just enough off the beaten track to keep the crowds away, but still easy enough to get to. Funny how we both ended up here. How'd you hear about this place?"

"Peter. I was telling him I wanted to do some camping this fall and that I hadn't spent much time in the southwestern part of Oregon. He gave me a list of his favorite campsites. How'd you find it?"

"I've come through here for years. My brother-in-law lives in Gold Beach on the coast and when my wife and I went to visit we'd always spend a few days camping. I'm on my way there now. My niece is getting married this weekend."

"Do young people still get married?"

"Apparently. The optimism of youth I guess."

"Will they never learn from our mistakes?" Claudie caught a slight grimace on his face and too late remembered that Nathan was a widower. "Not that everybody made the kind of mistakes I'm well known for." Not that anybody should be ashamed of a regrettable early marriage. That's why they called them starter marriages after all.

"Really? I must not get out enough. I've heard nothing but good things about you. Peter always has nice things to say about you when he comes into the bookstore."

"I'm glad to hear it. I'm a big fan of him too. Living next door to him and his kids is like having a ready-made family. I never had kids of my own. Do you have any?"

"Daughter. She and her husband live in New York." He finished his glass of wine and stood. "I'll let you finish putting up your campsite. If you need anything just yell."

Claudie watched him amble away and then set to work. In half an hour she had her air mattress blown up and her sleeping bag in place in the tent. The propane cook stove was ready, and she began preparing her dinner. When she was young, when she could backpack into remote areas, she had relied on freeze-dried food. Back in the '70s and '80s the culinary merits of 'backpacker food' was akin to hamster kibble. And although the variety and quality of the freeze-dried food had advanced, now that she only went car camping, she preferred to bring real food. Tonight was Columbia River salmon with fried potatoes, onions, and broccoli. Way too much for her, but she could have the rest for lunch the next day.

While the food was simmering on the stove, she hiked up the gentle rise to the outhouse. She was thankful that it was clean and relatively odor free. She hung the little cardboard tree deodorant anyway. She took the circular road on the way back so she could check out the other campsites. This took her past Nathan's RV. He was sitting outside on the picnic table with a bag of potato chips and a can of beer.

"I see that you are sticking with the basic food groups."

He looked down at the bag and then back up at her with a grin. "I hate all the packing and cleanup. I usually rely on convenience store crap. I see that you're cooking. You have remarkably high standards when it comes to camping. Good wine with real wine glasses, and a fresh cooked dinner. You're much more ambitious than I am."

"I don't know about that. It's just that I have a set way of doing things. My friends used to rib me. They called them 'Claudie Rules'. But they never turned down a dinner invitation either." She smiled and then started back to her site. No, no. No. Don't do it. Five steps. It would just encourage him. Ten steps. Claudie, you old fool. She turned and walked back. She paused, looking at him and the bag of chips. "I have plenty of food if you'd like to join me. It's the least I can do for you, helping me with the tent."

"Really, no big deal."

"I have Chinook salmon I bought and froze last spring from some Native Americans in the Columbia River Gorge."

Nathan whistled.

"Fried potatoes. Broccoli, but I won't make you eat that."

He laughed. "I like broccoli, but you had me at the salmon."
He stood and they walked back to Claudie's spot.

Claudie poured more wine and served the meal. Nathan
made appreciative groans as he started to eat.

"I don't know if I've mentioned how much I like your
bookstore. It's a little like stepping fifty years into the past.
How long have you owned it?"

"I bought it about six years ago. I was always going to
upgrade it but things got in the way. Now it's like an old
sweater, not sightly but very comfortable."

"I'm glad you never got around to it. What did you do before? Did you grow up around Sisters or Bend?"

"No. I grew up in Portland. I went to school back east and
ended up teaching at various universities."

"Such as?"

"The last one was in Lebanon, the American University."

"Wow, what did you teach?"

"Philosophy."

"Oh. That's interesting." It was one subject that Claudie
had avoided at her university.

"Not really. Most people change the subject when they hear
philosophy. Think it's too eggheaded or something."

"Well, I have to say I don't know much about philosophy.
My degree was in English Literature."

"Lots of philosophy in literature."

"Not the kind I read. At least anymore. So, did you have a specialty? Did you explore the meaning of life?"

"It's turtles all the way down."

"I beg your pardon?"

"It's an old philosophy joke. A Greek student asks his teacher, 'If Atlas holds up the world, what holds up Atlas?' The teacher says, 'Atlas stands on the back of a turtle.' The student then asks, 'But what does the turtle stand on?' The teacher says, 'Another turtle.' The student asks, 'And what does that turtle stand on?' The teacher replies, 'My dear, it's turtles all the way down.'"[1]

She laughed, "Ah, sounds a little like Terry Pratchett's *Discworld*. Any other answers to live by?"

"I didn't teach Metaphysics. I felt the big questions were beyond my ken. I specialized in the philosophy of mathematics. Logic and analytical thinking. And this is usually when people start drifting away at cocktail parties. I don't want to bore you."

"I have nowhere to go. Although I admit I don't understand much about it. I suppose that logic helps you win arguments, but probably at the expense of irritating a lot of people."

"Not as many as you'd think. Arguments, that is. I do irritate plenty of people. People don't want to have the fallacy of their positions pointed out to them. Certain people don't like facts to get in the way of their opinions."

....

[1]   See "Plato and A Platypus Walk Into a Bar", Thomas Cathcart

"It is true that there are facts and facts. Sort of like statistics, there's statistics and then there are damn statistics. Go on. Bore me some more."

Nathan chewed for a moment. "Okay. Don't blame me. One aspect I taught was paradoxes. There is a paradox called the 'Russell Paradox', named after Bertrand Russell. It goes like this: 'Is the set of all sets that are not members of themselves a member of itself?'" Nathan laughed. "Your eyes just crossed. Let me give you an example. 'If a man tries to fail and he succeeds, which did he do?' That, by the way, passes for humor in the philosophy set."

"Hmmm. I think I might stick with Douglas Adams answer to the meaning of life."

"42?"

"Yes, see you do know some of the big answers. I especially like Adams' great motto, 'Don't Panic.' It's useful in so many ways."

"Works for me. You're a very good cook by the way. This salmon is delicious."

"Thank-you. The wedding you're going to. Is it going to be one of those big fancy ones that people have now-a-days?"

"Fancy, I expect. My brother-in-law doesn't do anything by halves." Nathan chuckled. "King lives in a huge house overlooking the ocean. My niece mentioned parasailing, fireworks, and some famous singer, the name escapes me, singing at the wedding. Ellie, my niece, has tried to restrain him but he's a force of nature. You may even have heard of him?"

"Me? How?"

"You've heard about the amazing all-in-one grooming tool called 'The Wiz'? It's like the Swiss army knife of grooming tools. King invented it back in the '90s. It can dry your hair, curl your hair, straighten it if you want, pluck your eyebrows if you're so inclined, and God knows what else. He's called the 'King of Groom' on the late night home shopping networks."

"Not on my speed dial I'm afraid."

"Well, you wouldn't forget him if you had. King, his real name is Ben, is not a large man, but you wouldn't know it from hearing him. He's got this big booming voice that was made for the theater. In fact, he does community theater in the summer. His greatest role was Professor Harold Hill in the Music Man. My wife Kay, she was …" Nathan paused and looked embarrassed. "You know how some kids look like they sprouted from the same bush? Kay and Ben didn't look like they even came from the same planet. But enough. I've talked on too much. Tell me more about Claudie."

"Only if we can sit around a nice fire. Can you start one while I clean up?" It was a good way to avoid the topic. Claudie was no longer interested in talking about the past. It was too full of pitfalls not avoided, and doorways opened that should have stayed shut. She preferred to fly under the radar now. No more fuss in her life, thank you very much. Nathan was a doorway she wasn't going to open.

Chapter Two

Wednesday evening

The light had faded to a faint pink in the west and Claudie and Nathan were sitting in camp chairs in front of the small fire. The only sound was the gentle play of wind high in the Ponderosa pines, and the occasional gurgle from the nearby river. They were both lost in their own thoughts when gradually they became aware of the sound of a diesel truck coming down the narrow road to the campground. They watched as an old battered tan pickup pulled into the campground, it was pulling a long horse trailer.

"Too good to last. I hope it's not full of screaming kids."

"Don't worry, they won't stay. There's no spot big enough for that trailer. I've got the only one that comes close." They watched as the truck slowly circled the campground; it paused for a few seconds by Nathan's RV and continued on. The rumbling diesel engine filled the air with a layer of diesel fumes. Claudie couldn't wait for the idiot to move on to a better site.

"Shit." She glanced at Nathan, "Sorry, crap." The truck was circling around again, this time pausing by Claudie's car. In the dim light they couldn't see anybody inside the truck, but they knew that they were clearly visible to the driver. It crept on, again pausing significantly by Nathan's RV, and then moving on to a site on the curve of the gravel road.

"No way." Nathan stood to get a better view. "He can't fit in there. There's boulders bracketing the parking spot, it's too small."

Claude stood up to see. The driver had pulled past the spot and gotten out of the truck to look at the space. A black and white Border Collie jumped out after him and ran over to the closest tree and peed. The man climbed back into the truck and then began to back the trailer into the space. He didn't make it on the first try, or the second. On the fourth try, Claudie sat down. She hoped there weren't any horses in the trailer. She listened to the gears grind and there was an occasional scrape of metal, on the boulders she assumed. She poured a last glass of wine and resumed contemplating the dwindling fire.

She was startled out of her reverie when the dog walked into the firelight. He had his nose up sniffing the air.

"Hey, puppy. Are you hungry?" The dog waved his tail slowly and stared at her with large brown eyes. She patted her thigh and the dog hesitated for just a second and then came over and laid his head on her leg. She stroked his head and he lifted one paw and rested it on her leg. "Sorry buddy, you're a little too big for a lap dog."

Nathan glanced down and reached over to pat the dog but the dog avoided his touch, a low growl in his throat. Just then they were all startled by a loud crunch.

"He's jack-knifed the truck and managed to wedge the trailer into the rocks."

The truck was finally turned off and the driver got out to look at the situation. They could hear him begin to pound on something; each blow was accompanied by a booming curse. Claudie noticed that the dog was sitting on her feet now and she gently stroked his head.

"What's he doing now?"

"I can't see. Should I go up and help?"

"I wouldn't advise it. Somehow I don't think it would be appreciated."

One last curse detonated in the air and then silence. Nathan could see the man open the trailer door and go inside for a minute. He came back out holding a can of beer. He looked around and then called out for the dog. The Border Collie's head jerked on Claudie's lap and he looked up toward his owner. His ears went low and a low whine escaped his throat.

"He's coming this way." Nathan sat back down and waited.

"You guys see my dog?" The short stocky man walked past Claudie's car, the picnic table still hid the dog from his sight.

Claudie was conflicted. With no doubt in her heart, she knew that the dog was not happy with this man. But it was not possible to hide the dog and, before he could step closer and see it cowering down at her feet, she said, "He's here. I kept ahold of him while you were trying to park your trailer."

The man could see the dog now and his face twisted into an angry grimace.

"Get the fuck over here, you stupid meatball." He held his arm out, finger pointed menacingly at the dog. The dog cowered down and practically crawled over to him. The man grabbed his collar and started back to the trailer, yelling at the dog the entire time. They could hear the dog whining the whole way, but at least the man didn't hit it.

Claudie felt tears spring into her eyes and her heart was racing. What could she have done? She looked at Nathan and he was watching the man go, his face was rigid and eyes narrowed. "I want to shoot people like that. Do you think we can report him?" she asked.

"Report what? Guys like that get away with abusing their animals all the time. According to the law, the dog is just a piece of property. He can pretty much do what he likes with it." Nathan gave a disgusted shake of his head. "I'm sorry. What a horrible end to a pleasant evening." He looked over to the truck and then back to Claudie. "Are you going to feel safe tonight?"

"I'll be fine. I always keep a revolver by my pillow when I camp alone. Nothing gets into my tent that I don't invite."

"A handgun? Don't tell me on top of your other talents you're a crack shot? Former assassin in another life?"

"Was it that obvious? I'm hiding out in Sisters till the evil gangsters I double-crossed think I'm dead. Actually, I used to go to a gun range. I know it's not politically correct, but I like shooting. I just wouldn't shoot anything that breathes. Anyway, it's been a number of years since I shot anything." She smiled.

"Good for you. It's probably a good idea to have a little insurance. I doubt that cretin is going to do anything else except drink a six-pack tonight. Well, thank you for the excellent dinner, Claudie." He hesitated, and for an instant Claudie thought he was going to hug her. "Maybe I can fix you a cup of coffee in the morning?"

"That would be nice, but I'll bring a teabag for myself."

"It's a date." This time he did give her a hug; it was over before she could respond. And then he walked back to his RV.

Claudie stood for a few minutes. Brief as it was, it was nice to be hugged. She liked the feel of his body. He was still lean and hard, not squishy like some older men. She shook her head. God, she was so easy. Let a man look at her in a certain way and she got all gooey. Damn it, she told herself she wasn't going to get involved and for once she was going to listen to the wiser voice in her head.

She stirred the fire down and then poured a bucket of water on the coals. She stirred it again to make sure it was entirely out. She was a real stickler about campfires. That was another one of her rules. She'd seen too many people drive off with their campfires still burning and smoking. If she'd had her way they'd spend a night in jail.

She looked up at the trailer. She couldn't see the dog but the man was building a huge fire. He apparently had given up on getting his trailer out of the tight grip of the boulders, and didn't seem concerned that his truck was blocking the narrow campground loop. Claudie sighed. She hoped that he'd take care with that fire. The woods were still summer dry, and it wouldn't take much to start a forest fire. She went into her tent and, with thoughts of Nathan, drifted into a light sleep.

Nathan couldn't sleep. He could see the man's fire through his tiny bedroom window. The idiot had built a bonfire and it threw off a hurricane of sparks every time he tossed a new log onto it. Nathan went out to the little kitchenette area and drank a glass of water. He decided to take a walk. From past experience he knew a sweet spot a little way up the road where his cell phone could pick up and send texts. The signal was too weak for a phone call but the texts went through just fine. At the door he hesitated and then went back and took a flashlight out of a drawer. There was a second phone in the drawer and he pocketed it too. It was a burner phone that he only used to communicate with his friend Dani. It had been a while since Dani had contacted him but he wanted to let her know that Ellie was getting married in a few days. On a vacation in Rome, Dani had helped him get Ellie out of what could have been a disastrous jam. Ellie probably never knew how close she and her friend had come to running off with the wrong kind of bad boy Euro trash. The kind who tricked young tourists into dangerous situations. Situations that scarred a girl for life. Dani had disposed of the boys, he never asked her how, and Ellie only suffered a day or two of minor heartache.

The moon was up now, about three quarters full, and lit up the road well enough that he didn't have to use his flashlight. He turned right at the campground entrance. To the left the road wound its way back to the county road. To the right the forest road went another ten miles before dead ending at a trailhead that backpackers used to get away from the riffraff car campers and RVs. About a quarter of a mile up the road he crested a small hill and that was where the first bar on his phone flickered.

Ellie had sent him a text about bungee jumping with her fiancé Eric. He laughed. It was like Ellie to think her Uncle Nate could keep up with her young friends. Ah, to be twenty-eight again. He smiled to himself. He didn't know why, but Claudie made him feel young again. Well, younger. Young enough to want to spend more time with her, to become close and not just in a friendship kind of way. But he could tell that

Claudie was not in the same frame of mind.

He texted Ellie back politely declining the bungee jumping excursion. He told her he did have a surprise for her, that he'd show her when he got there on Friday. He turned the phone off and pulled out the burner phone and powered it up. There were no messages in the inbox. He sent Dani the particulars about the time and place of the wedding and that he was camping. He'd be in Gold Beach on Friday. And then, on an impulse, he texted that he'd made a new friend. Someone Dani would approve of. He sent the text off and turned to go back.

He heard a vehicle turn into the campground. It must have been pretty long because it seemed like the driver had to back up and try again. It took him three tries. Nathan wondered what was going to happen when he found the jack-knifed truck blocking his way. Two idiots trashing his quiet camping experience. He imagined Claudie was probably revising her resolution to not shoot anything that breathes.

At the campground entrance he could hear the two men shouting. No, he realized that it was just one man berating the other. Nathan decided to walk down to the river and wait till the commotion died down. He found a flat rock and watched the dark water glide by under the milky moonlight. The river drowned out the campground brouhaha.

Chapter Three

Wednesday night

Sprocket threw another log on the fire and opened another can of beer. He sat down on the picnic table and worked on his excuses. His brother Hammer was going to be joining him soon and he wasn't going to be happy about the kink in their plans. A sense of dread began to grow as he waited. Sprocket never knew what was going to set off his brother. Sometimes the littlest of things, like the toilet paper going the wrong way on the toilet roll hanger could send him off on a tirade. Sprocket was pretty sure that screwing up the trailer would be considered a major fuck up. They needed to transfer the dope to an anonymous vehicle to drive it down to the meeting place outside of Yreka. He didn't know how long it would take Mindy Lou to discover the truck was missing and report it to the sheriff. All he knew was that they needed to be long gone before that. Mindy's temper was only marginally better than Hammer's.

Shit, he'd screwed up the only part of the job he was entrusted with. The simplest part for the simplest fool as Hammer had said. He threw another log on the fire. Damn, he should have gone back to the county road where he could pick up a cell phone signal. But, he had been soooo sure he could squeeze the trailer into the spot. Fuck. If that stupid old man hadn't taken the only large space, he wouldn't be in the fix he was in. Old farts like that should stay put in the nursing home. Better yet, die. His dad had the decency to kick off before he became senile. Although, trying to dig that old tractor out of a muddy field wasn't the way that Geordie Head would have freely chosen to go. If he had just remembered to block off the wheels to keep it from rolling over his head, things would have been different. But when it's your time, it's your time.

Sprocket looked around for the dog; he could see him curled up under the trailer. The damn mutt. The stupid dog slunk around the house and peed on the rug every time he looked at him cross-eyed. He couldn't believe Aileen had left the dog behind when she ran off with that guitar player, Oleg. Shit, whoever heard of a guitar player named Oleg? The guy was too stupid to even come up with a better stage name. If he wasn't hoping that Aileen might come back, he would have dumped the dog a long time ago.

Above the sizzle of the fire he could just detect the sound of a large vehicle coming down the road. It stopped at the campground entrance and then backed up to make the turn. It took about three tries to maneuver the twenty-six-foot truck onto the camp road. The diesel engine ground its way toward Sprocket's campsite, pausing a few seconds by the silent RV parked in the good spot. It stopped on the road, blocked by Sprocket's jack-knifed truck.

The driver's door opened and Sprocket could hear his twin brother haul himself out with a mighty grunt. He could see Hammer in the firelight, standing for a few moments looking at Sprocket's truck and then walking around it. Hammer ignored his brother and slowly walked along the trailer, noting how thoroughly wedged in it was between the rocks.

"It's not my fault. I can explain. This old asshole took the only good spot." He rushed his words but Hammer interrupted before he could explain further.

"What's to explain? You had only one thing to do. Meet me up here so we can off-load the stuff, and then you could drive it on to the buyer." Hammer paused significantly, and Sprocket waited uneasily for what, as sure as piss follows beer, would come next. He didn't have long to wait.

"What the hell were you thinking? No, excuse me, that's not fair, is it?" Hammer's voice began to build in the still night air. "Thinking is not one of your strong points is it? What you're good at, what I can rely on you for, is to F★★★★★G F★★K UP EVERY F★★★★★G THING I EVER F★★★★★G ASK YOU TO F★★★★★G DO. JESUS F★★★★★G CHRIST." Hammer slammed his hand against the trailer and the dog slunk into the shadows.

"This was the only spot open. The good one was taken by that RV."

"Why didn't you call me? We could have met up at another campground."

"There's no cell coverage up here, Hammer. I think the two of us, we can get the trailer unstuck."

Hammer didn't reply. He walked around the truck and trailer again, examining the parts of the trailer hooked onto the boulders. Silently he went back to his truck and opened a toolbox behind the driver's seat. He extracted a large sledge-hammer. The next ten minutes the campground rang with the sound of the sledgehammer smashing into the edge of the trailer. Sprocket watched hopefully, and when Hammer pointed to the truck, he started it up and began to straighten it out. Every attempt to un-jackknife the truck only made the trailer situation worse. He felt a sickening lurch in the trailer behind him and stopped when Hammer screamed at him. He got out to look. Hammer stomped around the campsite, inarticulate howls flying into the darkness. Sprocket knelt down and looked at the rear wheel of the trailer. It was at a funny angle, and he could see underneath that the axle looked broken. Fuck.

He stood and walked out of the firelight. It was best to let Hammer run down a little before they talked about what to do. The other two campsites were dark and silent. He wondered what the two old people were thinking. It was their fault. Sprocket hoped the old man was shivering in his bed in his nice new shiny RV. Sprocket paused and concentrated on a thought. He turned and went back to Hammer who was now sitting with a beer and staring into the dying fire.

"Hammer, I got an idea."

After about a half hour, Nathan was cold. When he stood he noticed a slight vibration in his pocket. He pulled out the burner; Dani had sent him a text.

Hi, old fart. Don't go camping on the coast. Big 'flash' biker rally around Pistol River. Illegal and dangerous. Nasty boys. Stay away. Glad to hear about Ellie.

He texted back a short message, "*Got it. Stay away from nasty boys.*" Then he headed back to the campground. If it was quiet he thought he could sleep. The bonfire was still going strong but he didn't see either of the men. He stepped into his RV and stopped short. A man was standing by the little kitchen sink; one of the cabinets was open and the man was holding the Glock 39 that Nathan had hidden under a bowl. Nathan opened his mouth just as something very hard smashed down on the side of his head.

Hammer looked down on Nathan's slumped body. "Help me

toss him out." He looked up and saw Sprocket still holding the gun. "Here, give that to me."

Sprocket held the gun out, barrel first, and Hammer pushed it so it was not pointing at his chest. "Shit, Sprocket, that's not how you hand a gun over. You could have shot me." Hammer took the gun and tossed it on the passenger seat in the front of the RV. "What are you doing?"

Sprocket had lifted Nathan and deposited him in the Captain chair behind the driver's seat. "I'm getting him out of the way. Jeesh, Ham, calm down."

"You need to get him out of the way *outside*, dummy."

"Don't call me dummy. The old man's hurt. We can't leave him out there in the cold, he'll freeze. Unless you want to add murder to our list of crimes."

"Fuck. I don't intend on getting caught so I don't care what's on some shit list. Stop acting like Florence Nightingale and help me dump this junk out of the cupboards. We need to get as many marijuana bricks stored in this heap as we can. I don't think it's all going to fit." Hammer picked up a roll of duct tape that was on the counter and tossed it to Sprocket. "Here, rope the old man up. We don't want him waking up and wandering off while we're loading up."

Wednesday night

Claudie woke to the sound of the large truck chugging up the campground loop. She listened as the shouting and banging unfolded; she could feel her body tense with anger at the ya-hoos who were so rudely ruining her sleep and camping trip. After one sustained unintelligible burst of fury it was silent. She really had to pee and debated going to the outhouse. She didn't want to get anywhere near the angry men though. She crawled out of her sleeping bag and stood in her long underwear looking out the tent door. It faced away from the road and the other campsites. The moon was behind some clouds and it was very dark. She waited for her eyes to adjust. She didn't want to use her flashlight; it would draw attention to her. There was a tree approximately five paces in front of her—it would shield her. She had a couple of tissues in her hand and stepped out. She could hear two men talking, but they had stopped yelling.

She cautiously made her way to the other side of the tree, squatted, and peed. She was pulling up her pants when she saw a flash of white near her picnic table. She froze. She heard a low whine, and could see that it was the black and white Border Collie. It was lying under the table looking in her direction. Poor thing. Then she immediately thought, Christ, they'll come looking for it. Well, not this time. She wasn't going to force this poor dog to go back to those low-lifes. No siree.

She approached the dog who watched her warily. She sat at the table and leaned down to look at the dog. She stretched her hand out and it gave her a tentative sniff. "Come on, buddy. Let's put you someplace safe." She glanced from her tent to her car and decided the car might be best. She patted the dog's head and murmured softly to it, trying to coax it out from under the table. Slowly it crawled out and sat on her feet, leaning back against her legs with his head perched on one knee. She stroked him and talked quietly, telling him he was just the bestest boy. She could hear the men talking now. She better do this quickly. She moved the dog off her feet, and then slowly started to walk it to her car. Damn. Her car keys were in the tent. Switching course, she walked toward the tent.

"Sit." She stepped into the tent and rummaged around in her duffle bag where she had dropped the car keys. Suddenly there was another loud bang and she froze. There was a rustle behind her, and she turned to find the dog lying down on her bed. Great, I hope you don't have fleas. She zipped the tent up again and sat down by the dog, putting a reassuring hand on its back.

"What should I call you, dog? You know, I think for now it's going to be Buddy. Right now I could use a buddy." Buddy leaned in and gave her a sloppy kiss. "Don't push it, Bud. I don't usually kiss on the first date."

She couldn't see what was happening out there but there was more shouting and banging. It seemed closer than before. She wondered what Nathan was doing. She hoped he was staying tight in his little RV. She reached under the edge of the air mattress and pulled out her revolver. Smith and Wesson, 38. An ex-husband had bought it for her. He had loaded scatter shot bullets in the chambers. He said it was so she could discourage an attacker while she brought her panic under control. Very considerate of him. But, she wasn't the panicky type.

There was relative quiet outside the tent. She could occasionally hear the men say something to each other, but she couldn't understand what they were saying. The dog lay quietly, and they listened in the darkness. Finally she heard a truck door slam and a diesel engine start up. This was followed immediately by the sound of another vehicle starting up. It sounded like they were moving down the road toward the entrance. She could hear them as they reached the road, one vehicle pulled away, but another one seemed to be idling. Then with a blast that made her and the dog jump, there was a gunshot. She held a hand to her rapidly beating heart and griped the gun tighter. She listened, but could hear nothing else except the idling truck grind into gear and head out toward the county highway. She sighed. Good grief, what excitement. She stood and unzipped the window flap facing out toward the road. She couldn't see anything, but the dog started a deep low growl, looking as if he could see monsters through the tent fabric.

"Quiet." The dog looked crestfallen and curled up on the sleeping bag again.

She couldn't hear anything now. It was going to be a great war story to share with Nathan in the morning. Now, if she could only go back to sleep.

Chapter Four

Wednesday afternoon

The door of the bar opened and Dani stood silhouetted against the hot sunshine for a minute before it closed behind her with a bang. If she had wanted to be subtle about her entrance, she failed. But she wasn't interested in being subtle. Not with this crowd. Men, mostly very large men, in leather vests, tattoos, and straggly hair sat at the bar or played pool in the back. There was a scattering of women hanging on beefy arms; except for their smaller size, they blended in with all the leather and ink and messy hair. The men stared at Dani with interest and the women stared with narrowed and contemptuous eyes.

Dani's eyes adapted to the dimness as she scanned the room looking for the one she wanted. He was in the back playing pool with the one she knew as Tommy. The gang leader Mark was sitting at a small table watching. Her target had glanced up at her when she came in but was now concentrating on a bank shot.

"Zach!" She pitched her voice to carry through the crowd's noise and it cut through like a knife in butter. Zach scratched his shot and stood glaring at her. Behind the glare was a shimmer of worry. Mark and Tommy looked at her with lazy curiosity.

She pushed her way toward Zach and at the last second leaped up and wrapped her arms and legs around him. At first he stood there still holding his cue and looking around at the mass of curious faces.

"Oh, Zach, I've been looking everywhere for you, you rotten wanger." That was said for the benefit of the room. For him, she put her mouth to his ear and whispered, "Put your fucking arms around me, *Brian*, or I'll tell everyone that Stephen is pining for you in your honking big bed."

He stiffened and then the cue stick dropped on the floor with a loud crack and his arms went where they were told. He tightened his grip and a little puff of air escaped Dani's lips.

"Easy does it, cowboy. Call me Dee and kiss me hard."

Again he did as he was told and when the mouth clinch was over they stood there a few seconds looking at each other. No hint of true love leaked from those eyes.

"You going to introduce us, asshole?" Tommy leaned against the pool table. He never took his eyes from Dani, his eyes speculative in his examination of her.

"Hey, I'm Dee. That's short for Deirdre but only me mum calls me that." She grinned at him, her arm firmly wrapped around Zach. Mark said nothing but he was watching them with narrow dark eyes.

"You been holding back on us, Zach. You never said anything about having a pretty little piece of ass like this. Where you been hiding Dee? You don't exactly sound like you're from around here."

"It's not his fault. I had to take off, me mum in Glasgow was sick and I went home to help out."

"Aren't you just a little angel?"

"Yeah, well this little angel has some shagging to catch up on." Zach/Brian pulled Dani toward the back door that led to the alley. Dani screamed a peal of laughter that cut off as soon as the door shut behind them.

He kept his grip on her as they passed twenty or so Harleys till they were half a block up the alley and in the dark shade of a giant cottonwood tree.

"Who the fuck are you? What do you think you're playing at?"

Dani shrugged out of his grip. "I'm not playing. I need to find some things out and I don't have time to try to worm my way in with these creeps. Particularly since it would probably involve fucking one or more of them. The 'ick' factor was too high. And there you were already embedded and I knew I wouldn't have to fuck you to get in with the gang."

"What the hell do you think you know about me?"

"Besides the fact that your boyfriend is impatiently waiting for you back at ATF headquarters? I know that you are investigating the biker gangs in Northern California. You are primarily concerned about gun running and drugs and the possibility that this little group is about to form an alliance with a major gang out of Detroit."

"How the fuck do you know these things?"

"The ATF computer system is not only out of date, but its security system is a joke. It was one of the easiest hacks I've done in years. And Brian, Stephen is real cute but you really shouldn't have those kinds of pictures on your phone."

"I could have you arrested."

"I doubt it would be before I sent those pictures out to your buddies in the bar. That would ruin a year's worth of undercover work and it *absolutely* would make you persona non grata at your agency."

"What is it that you want?"

"Hmm. I just want to hang with you and your buddies for a while."

"Cause you like them so much. What else?"

"Don't worry, I won't screw up your setup. Besides, I make good cover for you. Some of those girls back there were beginning to talk about you. Biker chicks don't hold anything back and some of them thought you were less than an enthusiastic sex partner."

"Again, what is it that you want?"

She smiled and then took both her hands and mussed his hair. He swore and slapped at her hands. She mussed her own hair and then pulled her tee-shirt out of her pants and indicated that he should do the same.

"Come on, hot stuff, put a smile on your face. We gotta look like we just had a quick shag. Be grateful, I'm rehabilitating your image. Zach followed her back to the bar. Cat calls and whistles greeted them as they went in, the door slammed shut behind them.

Chapter Five

Thursday morning

Claudie woke, not to the sounds of birds in the forest, but to the chugging of a diesel engine turning into the campground. She groaned. The yahoo had come back. She crawled out of the sleeping bag and unzipped the window facing the rest of the campground. A hulking black tow truck drove by, way too fast in Claudie's opinion, and screeched to a halt by a white delivery truck that was parked in a space a couple down from Nathan's. Wait. Where was Nathan's RV? His site was empty. The yahoo's site still had the trailer crammed between the rocks and next to it was the new truck. A tall woman with wild long black hair got out of the tow truck and slammed the door. She walked over to the back of the white truck and opened the back doors. Claudie could hear a scream, it was not a happy kind of scream. The woman was clearly enraged about something. A barrel-chested man climbed out of the tow truck driver's seat and stood looking into the back of the truck.

Claudie realized she was cold and quickly got dressed. She pulled on an old sweatshirt with a Sierra Club logo and stepped out into the cool morning air. First things first was put water on for tea and then hike to the outhouse. The dog followed her up the slight rise to the toilets and waited outside the door till she came out. The tow truck was just leaving and the campground was finally quiet. Thank God, Claudie thought. She walked over to where Nathan's RV had been but there was nothing to see. It seemed so odd to her that he would have just pulled out in the middle of the night. He didn't seem the kind of man who'd leave a woman alone in the woods with a couple of thugs parked next door. Not that she was helpless. She had made a point of that to him last night. Still. She caught a whiff of smoke and went over to the yahoo's fire pit. There were still live embers in it. Of course the idiot didn't put his fire out totally. She went back to her site, turned the fire off the kettle, and then filled a bucket with water from the nearest water pump. She hauled it back to the fire pit and poured it in. Steam and ash billowed out and she stepped back, nearly tripping over the dog. He was being a bit of a nuisance; she now knew where the expression "dogged his footsteps" came from. She picked up a stick and stirred the coals to make sure everything was out. There was something in it that wasn't from burning wood. She bent and could see a melted pen, what looked like a couple of batteries, and on the edge, a black leather pouch. She nudged the pouch out of the ring and picked it up. It was scorched, but not burned, and she opened it up. It was stiff from the fire and inside was some business cards. She pried one out of its slot and was startled to see it was for Nathan's bookstore in Sisters. What in the world was it doing in the cretin's fire pit? There was another pen lying in the dirt about a foot away. She picked it up and read the logo for Nathan's bookstore. Something was not right. She wanted to get away from this place and try to figure it out.

The tow truck roared back up the road and stopped again by the white delivery truck. She could see lettering on the truck door, "Hoyt's Auto Repair and Towing." The driver got out and climbed into the cab of the delivery truck. The woman hopped out and immediately came over to where Claudie was still standing by the drowned fire pit.

"Howdy. You been camping here for long?" Up close Claudie could see strands of grey in the woman's hair. Her face was narrow and long and her large dark eyes anchored a significant nose. She was wearing a denim jacket over a red plaid shirt and farmer's denim overalls. There was a feed store hat perched crookedly on her head. Claudie thought she was just missing a piece of straw between her teeth. She looked friendly enough, if somewhat agitated.

"I came in last night."

"You see the guy who drove that white truck?"

"No. It came in after I went to bed."

"That's my farm delivery truck. I was shipping my farm crop up to Portland this morning but someone stole the truck last night. Thank God I put a GPS tracker on it. Did you hear anything unusual?"

"Oh yeah. It was quite the night. Come on back to my spot. I need to make my morning tea. My name's Claudie, by the way."

"Mindy Lou."

"Hoyt, come on down here, this lady was here last night. She was just about to tell me what she saw." Mindy Lou turned to Claudie expectantly. Claudie told them about the pick-up and trailer getting wedged between the rocks. They wanted a complete description of the man and his truck. She did her best. She really needed tea so she started the kettle going again as Mindy Lou and Hoyt discussed who the man could have been.

"It had to be Sprocket. He drives an old tan pick-up."

"Sprocket doesn't have the brains to pull something like this off."

"Hammer probably put him up to it."

"Yeah, dumb and dumber. You add the IQs of those two idiots and you still don't have someone who could pull off a multi-million-dollar marijuana hijacking."

"There has to be someone else involved. Who have they been hanging around with?"

"What about Dwight? Isn't he a distant relation or something?"

"Now, Mindy Lou. We know you've had it in for Dwight since he ran his pick-up into your front porch last fourth of July, but we can't go hunting for him based on that. We got to ask around. See who's been seen with them."

"We should probably notify the sheriff. If you want to collect any insurance on this, Mindy, you're going to have to file a report."

"*Hell.* What I want is to shoot the little peckers who did this. If we get my crop back, then I say bury the dead and move on. Marijuana may be legal in Oregon now but that don't mean the insurance company and the feds are going to help us. And no sense getting the sheriff poking around getting underfoot. I don't want to have to worry about the niceties if we have to get harsh with those boys."

"I've got my guys patrolling the Agness Road in case they headed to Gold Beach."

"They packing their guns?"

"You bet."

"I sent word out to some guys I bike with. They're heading down from Portland, keeping their eyes open."

Mindy Lou and Hoyt drifted back to Mindy Lou's truck and Claudie could see them open a map. They were working on their strategy. Good old farmer Mindy Lou grew marijuana. Hardly the kind of crop she would have figured for the god and guns crowd.

The locals sure didn't think very highly of law enforcement. Claudie knew that a couple of the counties in southern Oregon had not been able to pass public safety levies and that the county sheriffs were operating on skeleton crews. It looked like Mindy Lou and her friends were going to conduct the investigation themselves. Claudie could see rifles racked in the rear windows of both pick-ups. This little vigilante group was going to shoot first and ask questions later.

She looked down at the scorched black pouch she'd retrieved from the fire. She didn't know why she hadn't mentioned Nathan. She was glad now. She was sick to her stomach thinking that Nathan might have somehow got in the middle of all this. She needed to talk to a real sheriff. If these mini-commandos found the RV, she had the feeling they wouldn't wait to sort out who was guilty or not. Not till the smoke cleared away. She tossed her tea, now cold, and began packing. Three more pick-ups rolled into the campground in the next thirty minutes. The posse was getting pretty large.

About an hour later, as she turned onto the county road heading toward Merlin, the car started steaming. Claudie pulled over and waited for it to cool enough for her to take a peek. Of course, her looking at it was not going to achieve much since car mechanics was not one of her skills. She had just opened the hood when the big black tow truck drove by and parked in front of her. Hoyt climbed down and took a look at the engine. His head surfaced and he looked pointedly at her sweatshirt. "Couldn't get your Sierra Club friends to help you?"

"They're too busy hugging trees I guess."

Hoyt gave her a tight smile and told her what was wrong with the radiator.

"There's a bullet smack dab in the middle of the radiator."

She remembered that last big bang last night. One of the yahoos had shot her car. The jerks.

Chapter Six

Thursday early morning

"Where the fuck are you, you stupid douche?" Hammer was shouting into the phone. It was the third voicemail he'd left for Sprocket in the last ten minutes. He restrained himself from smashing the phone onto the steering wheel of the RV. He was parked in a little county picnic area on the edge of Mugginsville, California, west of Yreka. He had made good time on Interstate 5; it was still dark, an hour or so before dawn. He was waiting for the buyer to show, and hoping the guy would be late. The problem was, he didn't have the whole shipment. About 20 percent of it was in the back of Sprocket's truck,

and there was no Sprocket to be seen. He'd lost sight of
him after they had hit the interstate in Grants Pass. Hammer
tapped his fingers in a staccato beat on the steering wheel.
He glanced back at the slumped form of the old man in the
captain's chair behind him. The man had not moved since
he'd given him that little tap and tied him up. He sighed and
looked out the dark windows; he could make out the out-
lines of picnic tables ringing the little gravel road. No cars
had passed on the main road since he'd turned in. Then a few
minutes later an old pick-up, with one headlight out, passed
by on the county road. Hammer didn't know what the buyer
would be driving. The headlight vanished into the pre-dawn
darkness. Hammer lowered his head and bounced it once or
twice on the steering wheel.

There was no way out of it. He had to call his cousin.
Dwight was his cousin by his uncle's third marriage, and he
was the brains of the whole operation. He was the one who
had come up with the plan. Hammer knew it was because
of the feud between Dwight and his ex-girlfriend's mother.
Dwight had wanted to become part of Mindy Lou's marijuana business but Mindy Lou had shut him out. She had turned
her daughter against him and caused the blow-out argument
that had ended with Dwight crashing his Ford pick-up into
Mindy Lou's front porch on the fourth of July. Later, it was
only by chance that Sprocket was at the hardware store when
Jason had come in and picked up several rolls of plastic and
tape. Sprocket had told Dwight, and he knew instantly that

it meant the crop was about to be shipped. They then set up a relay team, watching the farm and waiting for the delivery truck to roll out the driveway. They followed it to where the delivery driver parked it overnight at Hoyt's auto repair garage. Sprocket was assigned the task of stealing a trailer and waiting for Hammer at the campground. Hammer had the most dangerous job of stealing the truck from the garage. Meanwhile, Dwight had established an alibi at Max's tavern by becoming spectacularly and publicly drunk. Hammer felt hyped. He needed a joint but not before the trade-off. He dug a beer out of the cooler on the passenger seat.

Hammer tried Sprocket once more but he still didn't pick up. With a deep reluctant breath Hammer punched Dwight's number. Same thing. It rang about seven times and then went to voicemail. Hammer hung up and then tried it again. If the phone was by Dwight's bed, then sooner or later he'd pick up and start yelling. It took four times, and the cursing was loud and inventive on the other end.

"Jesus, I hope this is your burner phone. Just what I don't need is you calling me the night the shit gets stolen. Hold on a minute. I gotta puke." Hammer could hear Dwight upchucking into the toilet and then a flush. He could hear water running for several minutes and then Dwight finally got back on the phone.

"Okay. Tell me what's going on."

Hammer began with the jack-knifed truck and the stuck trailer. He could hear Dwight's steady breathing, broken only by deep drags on a cigarette and the occasional 'fuck'.

"So, let me summarize. Instead of making a quick and un-observed transfer of the weed to a stolen and not very unique or valuable trailer, you two jerk-offs steal an RV worth what, a couple hundred grand, and rough up some poor old schmuck in the process."

"The RV ain't that valuable. It's one of those little ones, kinda beat up too."

"And the owner? The one who got a good look at the two of you. What about him?"

"Oh, he's fine. A little cut on his head is all when I had to clock him." He glanced behind him and decided now wasn't the time to tell Dwight that the owner had come along for the ride. Hammer began to sweat. "You don't need to worry about him. There's no cell phone coverage up there, and I shot the old lady's car."

There was a gurgled exclamation from Dwight's end.

"What old lady would that be?"

Ham told him about the old lady Sprocket had talked to.

"So, there are now two witnesses to your little fuck up. Jesus." Dwight took a big breath. "Hold on." Hammer could hear him in the bathroom again.

When Dwight came back, Hammer spoke first. "Ah, Dwight. We did the best we could. We improvised."

"From this end it looks like you guys dug yourself into a hole. Okay. This has all been very enlightening. I'm glad you kept me informed. But where the hell are you? It's four and you should be at the meet-up place."

"Yeah, I'm here. The guy hasn't shown up yet. Which is good."

"Good? How come it's good that the buyer isn't there yet? It was supposed to go down by now."

'Yeah, the problem is the RV. Like I said it's one of those small RVs. We couldn't get all the stuff into it. I mean, I'm practically driving with it sitting on my lap as it is. So we improvised."

Dwight groaned.

"We loaded about a fifth of the stuff into Sprocket's truck. He followed me down. At least, he was supposed to follow me. He's not here. I don't know if he's lost or what. I can't get him to pick up his phone."

Deeper groan.

"Where'd you lose him?"

"Just outside of Grants Pass. He said he wanted to get a tarp to cover the back of the pick-up bed. He may have gone to his house to get it. Nothing's open this time of night. Plus, I wanted him to load up my motorcycle. I'm heading east as soon as we split the money."

"He went home with a load of weed sitting in the back of his truck? Are you two insane?"

"Dwight …"

"Shut up. It was a rhetorical question. I already know the answer. Let me think."

Dwight lit another cigarette and went into the kitchen for

a beer. It was definitely hair of the dog time.

"Okay. I'm going to call the buyer to get squared away on that. Sit tight. Then I'm going over to check out Sprocket's place." He disconnected and called his buyer. The asshole was still down in the Sacramento area eating breakfast at a Denny's. Good. Dwight told him not to hurry. He finished the beer and would have dressed, except he was still dressed from the night before.

It took him about twenty minutes to drive over to Sprocket's house. The truck wasn't there, but all the lights in the house were on. He parked his red Malibu and went up to the door. The door was slightly ajar and he pushed it open. Music was blaring from a TV in the living room but other than a couch rescued from a roadside dump site, there wasn't anything else there.

"Hey, Sprocket. Bro. You here?"

Dwight walked into the small kitchen and found the floor littered with smashed dishes and silverware. There was an overturned chair, and the room smelled of old pizza and spilled beer. He wasn't sure if it was Sprocket's usual style of better housekeeping, or a sign of things not being what they should. The back door was wide open and he looked out. In the light from the doorway he could see the backside of Sprocket's body. Beside him was a cast iron skillet that looked like the guilty weapon. Dwight hesitated. He wasn't close to his cousin, but seeing his dead body was a little sobering. Of course, Sprocket could still be alive, and therefore able to tell him where the fuck the truck and weed were.

"Ahhh, shit." He bent over Sprocket and turned him over. To his relief Sprocket moaned deeply, and began flinging his arms around to ward off any further assault.

"Wow, dude. It's me. It's Dwight. Settle down."

Sprocket looked up at him blearily and then reached up and gently felt a very tender spot on the side of his head. His fingers came away with dried blood. He whimpered at the sight.

"Stop being a pussy. Where's the truck?"

"It's not here?"

"No. What the hell happened?"

Sprocket sat up and looked around. He picked up the cast iron skillet and stared at it dumbly.

"Spock. Earth to Spock."

"Don't call me that." He tossed the skillet into the yard and stood up. He swayed slightly and Dwight steadied him. "You know I hate it when people call me that, asshole."

"Oh boo hoo. Sprocket's got his feelings hurt. Meanwhile twenty percent of my weed is missing and I have a buyer that will not be amused. *Where's the fucking truck?*"

"*I don't know.* Aileen was here. We had an argument." He went into the house, pausing to survey the kitchen disaster and then on into the living room.

"Oh man, my head is killing me." He turned around and went into the tiny bathroom and poured out a half-dozen aspirins. In the kitchen he found an open beer on the counter, popped the pills, and gulped down the lukewarm beer.

Within seconds he belched loudly and went back through the house and stood on his front door step and looked around.

"Aileen was here and you two argued. Why would she steal your truck?"

"I don't know. She wanted her dog." He decided to sit on the front steps, the cool outside air felt better on his head.

"Are you telling me she stole your truck because of a dog? Why didn't you just give her the damn dog?"

"I don't have the fucking dog. I lost it. It's out at that stupid campground. Where we met up to load the pot." Sprocket closed his eyes at the whole ridiculous unfairness of the world. "Man, I need that truck to go to work on Friday. *Ooow.*"

Dwight felt only a little bad about popping him up alongside his head. Only a little bad. "We need that fucking truck because it has the fucking dope in it, jerk-off." He stared off into the night. "Okay, where could she have gone? All we need to do is find her and get the truck back. Call her and tell her where the dog is."

Sprocket stood and dug his phone out of the back of his pants and began punching numbers. The first set of numbers went to a disconnected line. It took him four attempts before he reached her voicemail.

"Hey, Aileen. Listen, my cousin is here and he needs …" Dwight grabbed Sprocket's arm and took the phone out of his hands.

"Sit down, Sprocket, you don't look so good." Into the phone he said, "Aileen, I found my coz Sprocket here in a pool of blood. He's not doing too good. Now, I don't usually like to get in the middle of other people's quarrels, but I really want to help you two out. So, if you get that truck back here in the next hour, I won't let him call the police and press charges. I'll even help him find your damn dog. Call me back." He disconnected and then looked at Sprocket with disbelief.

"Damn, how stupid can you get?"

"What?"

"You were about to say my name and that I needed something in the truck. Did it occur to you that she'd immediately go looking for it? What's she going to do if she finds the dope? Do you think she's going to hand it over just to get her dog back?" He jumped when the phone rang in his hands. "That was quick. If we're lucky she hasn't found it."

"Aileen, darling." He twisted away from Sprocket who was trying to take the phone from him. "Sure, I can do that." He put the phone on speaker and Sprocket stopped lunging for it.

"Sprocket?"

"I'm here, honey."

"How's your head?"

"Shit, it hurts. I really wish you hadn't done that."

"Sprocket. It was the only way to get your attention. I still can't believe you lost Jasper."

"I know where he is, it's just that I can't get to him right now. My cousin and I are in the middle of this business deal, and that's why we really need that truck, honey."

"Sure, Sprocket. I can let you have the truck back. But if you want the stuff that was in the back, then you're going to go get my dog back, you asshole."

"Aileen. Aileen," Dwight broke in, "we're going to get your dog back. But we're under a bit of a deadline here and we need that truck. And what's in the back."

"No can do. You must be as stupid as that moron cousin of yours. Which cousin are you by the way? Sprocket must have about a hundred that I know of. Is this Packard? Anyway, dipshit, call me back when you've got Jasper. And don't you hurt a hair on his body or I'll dump this shit down the sewer."

"Fucking A. She hung up. Where's the fucking dog, Sprocket? We need to finish this clusterfuck and get this stuff down to Hammer." Dwight kicked the side of the house in lieu of kicking Sprocket's sorry ass down the steps.

"Come on, I'm taking you to my place and I'll head out to the campground."

He needed to give Hammer a call before he peed his pants. It was still going okay. Not according to plan but still okay. Don't panic.

Chapter Seven

Thursday early morning

Nathan regained consciousness somewhere just before Hammer turned off I5 in Yreka. They had used duct tape on his mouth, hands, and feet, and then wrapped it around his chest and the chair for good measure. He wasn't going anywhere soon. The blood had crusted on the side of his head where Hammer had clocked him. The pain was deep and centered behind his left eye. He had gotten lax. After all those years in Lebanon, and other more dicey places, he had left his RV unsecured. A child could have found the Glock 39.

He wiggled his jaw a bit, the three days growth of beard

had prevented the duct tape from adhering securely to his skin, and he worked to loosen it. He didn't want it to drop noticeably so he did just enough so he could talk or shout if needed. The majority of the space inside the RV was taken up with stacks of plastic-wrapped marijuana bricks. There wasn't any way he could get to his second, emergency revolver that was hidden under the sink. Pity. Hammer parked the RV in a small park and reached over to the passenger seat where he had a small cooler and pulled out a cold beer. He drank it down in three long pulls and then sat fidgeting for about fifteen minutes before he started calling. First his brother Sprocket, and then someone else called Dwight. Hammer was nervous and agitated. The trick was how to use that to his advantage. Nathan watched the single headlight of a truck go by on the road. He knew they were in northern California, an area referred to as the Emerald Triangle. Full of nasty boys. He could only wonder why thieves from Oregon would set up a drug deal in the middle of California's prime marijuana growing fields. Well, it wasn't hard to figure out. These weren't the brightest guys he'd come across. Yet, he was the one tied up. Not time to feel too superior. The truck with one headlight drove by again. A little slower this time.

"You do know that you're trying to do your deal in enemy territory?"

Hammer jumped a foot off his seat, giving Nathan a small amount of satisfaction. "What the fuck? How did you ...?"

"It's the beard. Duct tape can't adhere strongly to it. A

good thing too. I have a slight cold. I would have had trouble breathing. I assume you're not planning to kill me?"

"Don't be too sure, old man."

"The way I look at it, Hammer—you don't mind if I call you Hammer?—if your buyer doesn't get here in the next, say, thirty minutes or so, you're going to have an up front and probably hazardous to your health kind of confrontation with some local guys. They find out you're selling dope in their territory, they're going to be real perturbed. They're going to have a short and to the point discussion about the lack of respect that demonstrates to them."

"What the fuck? I didn't understand half of what you said, old man. Can't you speak plain American?"

"My name's Nathan. Sorry about the verbiage. I was a university professor. Big words were my stock and trade, so to speak. To be simple, you may have already attracted the attention of some other bad guys. They may be coming back. If they do, they will probably shoot at you. I don't like the idea of being in the middle of your shit. Is that plain enough?"

"Don't you worry about me, Professor, I ain't exactly unequipped for run-ins with other dudes. This here is one nice pistol. Where'd you get this? You sure don't look like someone who'd be packing a Glock. Even if it's a little bitty one like this." Hammer pulled the gun out from under his seat and waved it in Nathan's direction. Nathan pretended to flinch; unless the idiot had been playing with it there was no bullet in the chamber, so the deadly weapon was currently just a piece of metal. "Don't worry yourself, Professor, I ain't hit anything I didn't want to since I was ten."

"I have a question for you, Hammer. Why am I here? Why didn't you just leave me at the campground? I'm just unnecessary baggage. You could kick me out now and there wouldn't be any way I could muck up your plans."

Hammer snorted. "My dumb brother thought you'd freeze or something. Don't worry, Professor, I'm dumping you as soon as I can."

Nathan watched him closely. Hammer's eyes and forehead were scrunched in thought. Nathan assumed he was trying to figure out a way to get rid of the problem that was Nathan. A witness who could identify him. The thought that this idiot might decide on a lethal solution to his problem made Nathan highly uncomfortable. He'd have to help Hammer come up with a resolution that didn't end up with Nathan rotting in a shallow grave in the forest. There had only been one other time that he'd gotten in a jam, it was when he was "consulting" for a certain unnamed government agency. He kept his captor talking, trying to make himself human to a man who viewed non-believers as sub-human. That time of course, Dani swooped down and saved the day. He needed to let her know that somehow he'd tangled with some nasty boys. And in the meantime, as the great Chinese general Sun Tzu would have advised, "Pretend inferiority and encourage arrogance." The great thing about dumb people like Hammer, they never knew they were dumb. They always thought they were the smartest people around. Sort of like the Enron guys.

The conversation died down for a while. Hammer kept a close eye on the road. He could see pale pink in the eastern sky and as it got lighter he became increasingly nervous. It was an hour since the Professor had warned him. He jumped when the phone trilled.

"Dwight. Where is everybody? I'm getting a bad feeling about this place. I think someone's watching me."

"Don't be such a pussy. I can't have you breaking out in hives every time there's a hitch."

"Easy for you to say. I'm the one sitting here in broad day-light with a truck full of stolen marijuana, with maybe some of those backwoods California biker dudes sniffing around me. Where the hell are Sprocket and your guy?"

"The buyer should have been there an hour ago. I'll call him. Meanwhile, forget about Sprocket. He got detained, he isn't going to make it."

"Detained? What the fuck does that mean? I'm going to kill …"

"*Shut up.* I don't have time or patience for your shit now. Just hold tight, make the exchange, and head to the cabin like we planned. Don't forget to check the odometer when you turn on the road, one-point-nine miles exactly, on the right. And for God's sake, start texting me. The cell phone coverage is lousy up there. Texts can get through sometimes where a phone call can't."

"I hate texting. My fingers are too big."

"Christ, I showed you how to use the end of a pencil or something. I want updates on what's going on. Just do it."

"Oh, Jesus." Hammer dropped the phone and concentrated on the truck turning into the picnic area. The truck with one headlight out. The truck with what looked like two very large men. Men with tattoos and a shotgun in the rear window.

"Hammer? Hammer, what's going on?"

Hammer put the RV in gear and whipped around the outer circle of the picnic park and out the exit, his rear wheels slipping in the loose gravel before they got purchase on the asphalt. The thrill of escape lasted mere moments before the truck was on his tail. What Hammer learned in those moments was that the RV was not built for speed. He didn't know whether it was right or left to go back to Yreka. His sense of direction was haphazard at best. Maybe it would be better to try to lose the truck on the winding forest roads.

"Hey, Professor? You awake back there?"

"Oh yes. Shaken, but not stirred."

"What the fuck? Can you just give me a straight answer? Your fucking GPS isn't working, which way is the freeway? Right of Left?"

"Left. No, maybe right. Sorry, I get turned around easy. Let me think a minute."

"We don't have a minute, Professor. Lot of good you are in an emergency."

He looked in the side mirror and could only see the truck's

side mirror sticking out from the driver's side. There was probably only a foot or so between the RV and the truck. Hammer tried to nudge a little more speed out of it, when a small miracle happened. Coming round the bend in front of him was a highway patrol car. They passed so quickly that the driver of the truck didn't have time to register the unfortunate turn of events until the patrol car did a fast U-turn and put his lights and siren on. The truck backed off instantly and Hammer sped on. He could hear chirping coming from his dropped phone and finally picked it up.

"Dwight?"

"What the fuck is going on? Was that a police siren I heard?"

"Yeah. Never thought I'd be happy to see the police." Hammer started laughing in a hiccupping sort of way.

"Hammer! Get a grip. Tell me what happened."

Hammer told him about the truck with one headlight.

"Shit. Where are you headed now?"

"Not sure. West. Give me a few minutes to find a place to stop and look at the map." It was ten minutes before he found a turn out that the RV could drive in and shelter out of sight of the county highway.

Dwight hung up and tried calling the buyer. It went to voicemail so he left a message to not go to the rendezvous spot but to call him right away. His phone rang almost immediately.

"Sorry I missed your call, I was taking a piss. Hey, I can't find the place anyway. I'm looking at a map and I don't see no Mugginsville. There's a Kneeland, and a Loleta, that's east of here. And just north there's an Arcata ..."

"Jesus S. Christ. You drove to Eureka. I told you *Yreka*. Yreka, not Eureka. Dumb fuck Iowa farm boy." Instead of being a short distance from Interstate 5 the driver was now on the coast highway in Northern California, 75 miles south of the Oregon border.

"There's no reason to curse. I don't like it when the Lord's name is taken in vain."

"Excuse meeee. I had no idea I was dealing with such righteous people. You do know that you're picking up marijuana? What would your preacher think about that, Jesus boy?"

"My preacher knows that to sin is human, and that Jesus forgives all our sins so long as we believe that he is our savior. Have you let Jesus into your life?"

"Jesus. Listen, Iowa. I don't have time to discuss my religious and philosophical beliefs with a two-digit IQ like you. Tell me where you are right now and I'll call my driver and set up a new rendezvous."

"McDonald's."

"Which one? Unlike Pisspot Iowa, Eureka is going to have more than one."

Dwight could hear a heavy sigh on the other end, then the truck door opening and the sound of footsteps retreating. A minute later the footsteps returned and the door opened and slammed.

"Tenth and Fresno." Obviously the driver had decided to

keep the conversation short and to the point.

"Stay there till I get back to you. Have another breakfast. You Iowa folks probably eat as often as Hobbits."

"Who?" But Dwight had cut the line.

He called Hammer who had figured out that he was on Highway 96 headed toward Happy Camp, a dot on the map in the Klamath National Forest.

"Shit, man. I don't want to drive to Eureka. It's all mountain roads. It'll take me forever."

Dwight googled a map of Northern California and Southern Oregon. The roads to the coast were limited. He studied the various routes.

"Okay. There's a county road that goes north that will connect you to Highway 199 just inside the Oregon border. Then you have to go south to Crescent City. That's just a few miles into California. Find a McDonald's and I'll send him there. Then it'll be easy after the exchange to head north out of Brookings and get to the cabin."

"We can't exchange the goods in a McDonald's parking lot, Dwight."

"No shit, Sherlock. I just want you two to find each other. There's parks and forest all around that area. You two can find a good place together and get this whole fiasco over."

After Dwight had relayed the new rendezvous point to Iowa, he sat with his head resting on the steering wheel. His head felt like it had been used as a basketball in a pick-up game in the ghetto. He was exhausted, and he still had to get that damn dog for Aileen so he could get his dope back. He had already given up the idea of getting it to the Iowa buyer. There wasn't as big a profit for it in Oregon or Washington, now that it was legal. He'd probably have to go as far as Montana or North Dakota to unload it. It might not be worth it. He should let Aileen deal with it, but Sprocket was adamant about getting his truck back. Besides, if Aileen got caught and squealed, then sooner or later he'd be fingered. Sprocket wasn't dumb enough to lie that well. He had Sprocket stashed at his place. He needed to keep him out of sight till he had his money and was headed to LA. Then he didn't care what happened to those two losers.

By the time he got to the campground he had to keep on trucking. It was crawling with pick-ups and men with guns. Friends of Mindy Lou's no doubt. This was an unfortunate turn of events. How the hell did they find the truck so quickly? Bad luck. A quarter of a mile on Dwight backed into a gated logging road. There was no way out except going back the way he came. Dwight fretted over the delay and his inability to get a signal on his cell phone. Thirty minutes later, most of the trucks had left and Dwight decided to chance it. He drove swiftly past the campground and breathed easier when he hit the county road. A couple of miles down he could see a car pulled over to the shoulder. A woman and a black and white dog were standing beside the front of the car. The hood was up and a man had his head deep inside poking around the engine. Dwight sped by; his heart lurched when he realized who it was. Hoyt had stopped to help the old lady. He was driving his honking big tow truck. Fortunately Hoyt stayed focused on the engine.

Now he knew where the dog was, and if Hoyt towed the old lady to his garage in Merlin then he'd have an opportunity to grab it there. Don't panic.

Before Hammer could get the RV rolling again, Nathan requested a bathroom break.

"Piss where you are, Professor. I ain't cutting you loose."

"It's not just pee, Hammer. Do you really want me to shit my pants? I'm sitting right behind you, it's not going to smell pretty."

Hammer sighed. He could use a pit stop too; that beer went right through him.

"You've got a gun. We're in the middle of nowhere with no one around, and I'm not exactly spry anymore. What are you afraid of?"

"Not you, old man. You know, you aren't exactly in a position to mouth off at me like that, fucking dickwad. I should let you shit your pants, roll my window down and I wouldn't smell a thing, especially over the smell of the weed." He drummed his fingers on the steering wheel. Shit. He pulled out his pocketknife and reached back and cut the duct tape holding Nathan's legs together, and then the tape binding him to the chair. He quickly leaned back and picked up the gun. He opened the door and got out. The only way for Nathan to exit was to climb into the front and out the same way Hammer had gone. They stood for a moment looking at the nearby trees. Hammer waved the gun and Nathan walked a few feet to the nearest tree and did his business. Hammer was behind him, a strong steady stream hitting the gravel road.

"I thought you had to shit."

"I'll hold out for someplace with toilet paper."

"Suit yourself. Back in."

Hammer climbed in and started to look for the roll of duct tape. He started swearing again, he was coming up empty. He turned and glared at Nathan for a long minute.

"I should just pop you right now. Take care of a lot of problems."

"Easier to just kick me out of the RV. We're twenty miles from nowhere. You'd be long gone before I finally got any-where."

Hammer considered this for a couple of minutes. Then he thought of the guys in the truck. If they found the old man they might make him tell them where Hammer was headed. He was sure Nathan had overheard enough of his conversation with Dwight to know he was headed to Crescent City. It would be best to hold onto the old prick until the exchange was made and Hammer was safe on his way to Dwight's cabin. He could decide later if the old man was too much of a liability to let go. Bodies disappear in the forest all the time.

"I think you're going to sit there with your mouth closed until I decide where I'm going to dump you. And you better

behave yourself or you're going to be bleeding when I do."
He waved the Glock for emphasis.

Nathan nodded with his eyes shifted down and a defeated shrug of his shoulders. He didn't want Hammer to get nervous about him causing trouble. He'd achieved his goal; his body and legs were mobile, and when the time came his hands would be too. He could feel the burner phone against his hip. All he had to do was wait for his chance, and hope that the call went through. He wondered what Claudie was up to by now. Would she think it odd that he wasn't still at the campground? She was an attractive and perceptive woman. She was the first woman since his wife died that he'd been interested in. He liked her intelligence and sense of humor. Not bad looking either. She certainly didn't look like she was in her early sixties. But, she didn't seem to reciprocate his interest. She probably went to a different campsite and forgot all about his promise of coffee.

Chapter Eight

Thursday morning

"Jesus. Are you telling me you guys tracked this truck nearly two thousand miles and lost him at the last minute? What kind of amateurs am I dealing with here?" Mark started pacing around the sandy campsite that he'd established as their headquarters. Dani strained to hear him above the sound of the nearby surf. Tommy, Zach, and several others were huddled around a campfire watching their boss scream into his phone. A light rain had started to fall.

"If you'd told me where it all was going down I could have sent some guys to help ... What makes you think that the RV has anything to do with it? Probably just some poor schmuck camping with his family … So he ran? Could be he was just scared … Fuck … Okay, you take your guys and patrol I5 down to Sacramento and then head over to Eureka. I'll have my guys patrol Highway 101 from Gold Beach down to Eureka. If you haven't totally fucked this up we can talk about meeting at the Pistol River rally. What kind of RV was it?" He cut off the call.

"Tommy, I need you to take some guys and head on down the highway. Anybody know what a Minnie-Winnie is? Some kind of RV."

"It's a Winnebago, a little one."

"Okay. We're looking for maybe two vehicles. A white truck, maybe twenty-foot box with Iowa license plates. The other is a Minnie-Winnie with Oregon plates. Check out the campgrounds between here and Eureka. Call me as soon as you spot one and don't fucking lose them. Zach, I want you to take a couple of guys and head up to Gold Beach. There's a road that goes east toward Grants Pass and I5. You spot anything, call me."

"What are you going to do?"

"I'm going to try to find a fucking motel room. I'm not camping in this shitty rain."

A dozen motorcycles roared to life and drove up the horse trail that led back to Highway 101. Although she had been angling to spend some one-on-one time with Mark to try to inveigle some information out of him, Dani sat behind

Zach as he headed north. She needed to check on something. Nathan had a stupid Minnie-Winnie.

Chapter Nine

Thursday morning

Claudie and the dog got in the backseat of the tow truck and the large diesel engine roared down the road.

"So, Mindy Lou's truck was full of marijuana?"

"Yep. It had over two thousand pounds."

"Holy moly. That much?"

"Yep. Mindy's and two other growers. The entire season's worth. Those guys are going to be hurting. I wouldn't want to be Sprocket or Hammer if it turns out they were the ones who took it."

"Sounded like everyone at the campground was pretty

sure."

"I can't see Sprocket doing anything like that. Hammer, I don't know. I went to school with them, they're twins, the fraternal kind. Look a lot alike but different personalities. Sprocket is an okay guy, just dumber than a post. Hammer though, he's not too bright either, but he's a mean dumb with a hair trigger temper. He's been dragging Sprocket into one shit pile after another since they left school."

"How in the world did they get those names? They're a little unusual to say the least."

"That was their dad. My mom says he was plastered, drunk on his ass the night their mom went into labor. It wasn't an easy birth. She hadn't gone to the doctor and no one knew she was expecting twins. So it takes her awhile to recover, and by the time she's with it, Geordie had already filled in the names on the birth certificate. He always had a sick kind of humor."

They reached Merlin and he pulled up to his auto repair shop. In the garage he did more poking around the belts and hoses in the engine. "I can call around Medford or Ashland and see if I can run you down a new or used radiator. That should only take a couple of days, longer if I have to get it out of Portland." He stood and wiped his hands on his pants. "I hate to say it, but that may not be the only problem. You may have cooked a few gaskets when the engine overheated. Hard to say at this point."

Claudie nodded and recited a chorus of cuss words silently.

This was going to cost a bundle. Insurance might cover the radiator. Minus the deductible. But if the car had other mechanical problems, she doubted they'd be covered.

"Any chance you have a loaner car I could rent in the mean time?"

Hoyt nodded. "Sure. I got an old Subaru I could lend you. No charge. Just fill it up when you bring it back."

Ten minutes later, Claudie was looking at the loaner Subaru and thinking about gift horses. The car was a neon yellow Subaru Baja, of indeterminate vintage, but obviously many, many miles. Some of them looked like off-road miles. Scrapes and dents had been painted with primer, giving the car a spotted look. There would be no way she'd lose the car in a parking lot. She was surprised by a bumper sticker that read "Coexist" in a kind of runic script. It seemed a little out of character. It wasn't until she started loading that she took a better look. Each letter was formed by a weapon of some sort. The "o" was a grenade, the "t" a rifle, the "x" two crossed knives. That fit the local zeitgeist.

She transferred her cooler and other necessities to the yellow car. She needed to get something to eat, probably the dog could use some food too. She found a small café and ordered breakfast. It was the first moment of peace since Mindy Lou had rolled into the campground. She started thinking about the previous night. She wondered at what point Nathan had deserted her. It seemed even more cowardly, now that she knew someone had actually shot her car. What the hell was that about? Something just didn't seem to make sense. How could Nathan get mixed up with the idiot brothers? Or was he already halfway to Gold Beach for his niece's wedding? She needed to figure out her next moves. Maybe if she went to Gold Beach she could make sure he was there, safe and sound. Her imagination was getting a little manic.

Back in the Subaru she gave the dog part of her breakfast and then pulled out a map and tried to figure out the best way to go. In this corner of Oregon it was hard to get to the coast. Most people took the highway that dipped down into California and then headed up Highway 101 to the little towns of Brookings, Pistol River, and Gold Beach on the southern Oregon coast. There was a direct route through Agness but it was renowned for being difficult. In the winter, people had gotten trapped on it and died. But in early fall the road was still good and she thought she'd give it a try.

She was still parked when a dark green sheriff's car rolled to a stop beside the Subaru. The tinted window came down. The sheriff was a tired looking man in his fifties. He had a day's growth of hair on his face and he looked like someone who sat too much of the time.

"You the lady was camping at Big Bend Campground last night?"

"Yes, I had that unfortunate experience. My name's Claudie O'Brien."

"You were actually pretty lucky, Mrs. O'Brien. Those were some bad men at that campground." The sheriff turned off his engine and got out. One of the vigilantes must have spilled the beans to law enforcement. It was a relief to Claudie.

"I'd like you to tell me what happened. I need the best description you can give me about the man you saw and his truck."

When all the details of the night's events, including Nathan this time, had been described, the sheriff brought her up to date on the search. He had notified the Oregon State Police because of the stolen marijuana. The estimated street value was well over a million dollars depending on where it was headed. A lot more money if it was headed to the mid-west. They had searched Hammer Head's house and his brother Sprocket's, but there was no sign of either brother. The sheriff wasn't optimistic. In this part of the state, law enforcement was few and far between. He was about to get back into his cruiser when Claudie stopped him.

"There's one thing that's been bothering me. My friend I mentioned? I have a funny feeling about him leaving. I find it odd that he'd go without saying anything to me."

"You think he somehow got involved?"

Claudie shrugged. "I don't know."

"Have you called him?"

"I don't have his cell number."

"Well, as you said earlier, you really don't know him that well. Maybe he got tired of all the noise and just left. If you can get his number, give him a call. Call me if you can't reach him and still think something's wrong." He nodded at her one last time and drove off. He clearly had a lot on his plate with the theft. He wasn't going to waste any time looking for someone who probably wasn't missing in the first place.

She hoped the sheriff was right. She tried to remember more about Nathan's RV, but she couldn't even think what the make was, let alone the model. Maybe what she should do is call Peter. Peter and Nathan were friends. He could tell her if she was getting bothered over nothing. At least he could give her Nathan's cell phone number.

She called and Peter picked up on the third ring. She felt foolish as she told him about her worries. He asked about the local sheriff and she had to admit that he wasn't too concerned.

"I understand that I don't really know Nathan that well. It just seems out of character for him to leave the campground and leave me there with these two jerks."

"It doesn't seem right to me either, Claudie. But I do know that Nathan doesn't like conflict. He always goes out of his way to avoid a fight. But still, he's the biggest gentleman I've ever met. Doesn't seem real chivalrous to me."

"It's not like I'm some frail flower that needs protection. I told him I had my gun."

"You have a gun?"

"It's just a small revolver. I just take it camping. Makes me feel better about camping alone."

"I understand. Well, that could have made a difference. Maybe he was worried you'd shoot him if he came up to your tent in the dark. He figured you'd take care of yourself and he didn't want to hang around those two jerks."

Claudie sighed, "Yeah, you're probably right. I'm going to keep trying to call him anyway. You wouldn't happen to know his brother-in-law's name or address in Gold Beach do you?"

"No, sorry. Listen, I've got a call. You call me back as soon as you know something."

Claudie hung up. What Peter said made sense. She'd just keep trying to call Nathan. She'd probably sound like an idiot when she finally got him on the line. This just goes to show, it wasn't a good idea to get involved in other people's lives. Too much drama.

Chapter Ten

Thursday early afternoon

Hammer found Iowa sitting in his truck at the McDonald's in Crescent City. They started driving through town while Hammer brought Dwight up to speed. Then Hammer caught a glimpse of a pick-up with a single headlight following them. He panicked. He pulled into a gas station and watched to see what the truck was going to do. Traffic was slow in town; there were dozens of motorcycle going north. These were biker dudes, tattoos and chains, leather jackets with lurid club names on the back, lots of chicks too. He got a good look at the truck as it went by. The driver was a big man with a Mennonite beard and hat.

Next to him was his equally large wife in a blue dress and white bonnet that Mennonite women wore. It took a couple of minutes for his heart rate to slow down. That fucking old man had convinced him that he was being followed again. He needed to get some more duct tape and shut the Professor up. The Iowa driver was behind him filling up. Hammer mentioned the truck but the Iowa driver seemed to think Hammer was being paranoid. He asked Iowa to keep an eye on the Professor while he went inside.

Hammer didn't really need any gas but he could use some cigarettes and beer. He went into the convenience store and looked around. It was crowded with high school students who were avoiding the federally mandated healthy lunches their school district provided. He had to muscle his way to the counter, ignoring the girly protests.

In the RV, Nathan slipped his phone out of his pocket and turned it on. The Iowa driver was standing by the driver's door watching the traffic flow by and not paying any attention to him. The phone made its little beep that it was on, and Nathan glanced out at the driver. Still oblivious. He didn't think he'd get away with a phone conversation, so he sent a text to Dani. It was their secret code. Basically, "could use some help here". He noticed that there were two messages from his niece Ellie and one with Claudie's caller ID. Somehow she'd found his number. It cheered him a little to think she was worried about him. He put the phone on vibrate and slipped it back in his pocket about the time Hammer climbed back into the RV. Now he could only wait. Again he wondered what Claudie was up to. He had her phone number now, but he didn't want to text her. He didn't want to distress her, but he hoped that she had figured something was amiss. Maybe by now they'd found the stuff from his RV that the dunces had dumped. They'd wanted to cram as much dope into the RV as they could, and they had emptied out all the cabinets. The only thing not replaceable was the black leather pouch. But he probably would never need it again. It just felt better to have a fall back escape stratagem. Thinking of future escapes seemed silly under the circumstances. He needed a couple tricks to get out of this mess. Dani could be in the middle of something and not be able to help, or help in time. Now, how to fuck with Hammer's mind? Hammer was jumpy as a grasshopper in a cornfield in August. Paranoia made stupid people even more prone to do stupid stuff.

When he got to the truck, Hammer glanced back and caught one of the teenagers holding his camera up toward him. Hammer obliged with the one finger salute and got in the RV. He ignored the car waiting behind him and pulled out his phone. He'd try to leave a text. But the tiny screen and keyboard defeated him again. His cigar-like fingers kept hitting the wrong letters and he couldn't write a message that made sense. There was a loud honk behind him and he cursed and flung the phone down on the seat next to him. Fuck Dwight.

Back on the road, Hammer cracked another beer and

watched for signs to parks. He wanted to go east, away from the ocean. He figured he'd be more likely to find a deserted park to the east. They crossed back into Oregon and headed toward Harbor and Brookings. His phone rang. It was the other driver.

"No, dipshit, we're not going to drive all the way to Portland. Don't get your panties in a twist. Just outside Harbor there's a road that goes by a whole bunch of campgrounds. We can turn there and find somewhere to load you up." He had another call, so he switched to the other caller. It was Dwight's number, but the call was dropped before he could say anything.

The road to the campgrounds was coming up and he put his blinker on. It had started to rain and it was coming down hard, making it difficult to see. He watched to make sure the other driver followed him, and before looking back to the road he glimpsed two motorcyclists turn onto the road. Unease swept his body in another cold sweat. Shit, this job was going to be the death of him. He lit a cigarette to calm his nerves. He glimpsed the Professor in the mirror. Damn, he'd forgotten to buy more duct tape. The Professor was making a big show of looking out the side mirror. It was creeping him out.

He passed the first two campgrounds, watching to see if the bikers turned off. He didn't know how many miles the road went, or if it went anywhere other than deeper into the forest. His phone rang. It was the other driver but the connection was too bad to talk. There were four more campgrounds ahead. He thought he'd pull into the next one and see if the bikers followed. He slowed and turned into a narrow gravel road that curved to the right. He crept along, watching in his side mirror. Everything looked grey behind him, and he couldn't see behind the other truck. There were about ten sites in the campground; two were taken by other RVs. He circled the loop and then pulled back on the road. He couldn't see the bikers on the road. Either they were gone or they were right behind them. His grip on the wheel was hurting his hands. The other driver pulled in behind him and then lickety split two bikers followed. Fuck, fuck, fuck.

He didn't know what to do. He sure as hell didn't want to keep going farther into the forest. The bikers could trap them on a deserted forest road. He took the next campground turn and circled the loop, this time not bothering to look. Back to the road he turned west and gunned it. He wanted back to Highway 101 as fast as he could. The Iowa driver was right on his tail. One of the bikers gunned ahead of them and then slowed down in front of Hammer. He never even looked at Hammer, which was spooking him out. Who were these guys? Why'd they pick on him?

"Sure lots of bikers on the road."

"I'm not blind, old man."

"Wouldn't they love to find the marijuana in here? I suppose the sheriff and state police have broadcast the robbery on the police bands."

"*Shut up.*"

"Just saying."

They drove into Brookings where the traffic again crawled at a snail's pace. He tried to get Dwight, but it went to voicemail. He wasn't about to stop and try to send a text again. What to do? The biker in front of him pulled into a drive-in and Hammer watched to see if the other biker was going to join him. He let out a huge whoosh of air as he saw the other biker pull off. The next town was Pistol River and then it was Gold Beach. At this point, all Hammer wanted to do was make it someplace safe. He was going to drive to Dwight's cabin outside of Pistol River. The transfer would go down there. If Dwight didn't like it, then fuck him. He wasn't the one with possibly homicidal bikers on his ass. If there was going to be trouble, then Dwighty Boy was going to have a piece of it too.

"You're such a pussy, old man. No one's following us now. In a few more miles I'll be rid of the dope and you. You ever learn anything practical at that college of yours? You better pray that you picked up something about surviving in the woods, because where I'm going to drop you, you're going to have to be Daniel fucking Boone to find your way out."

Nathan continued to do what little he could to build on Hammer's paranoia. But as they say, you're not paranoid if someone actually is out to get you. The motorcyclists were not just fellow travelers. They had demonstrated way too much interest in the RV. They were shit for following unobtrusively, though. Hammer had spotted them. Nathan was surprised they were so brazen; it wasn't a good sign. Back on the highway, Hammer left two behind him but Nathan doubted that it would be the last they'd see of them. He had the feeling that there were more than the two riders. Dani had texted that there was a biker rally down here somewhere. Lots of nasty boys, she said. He wondered if the grapevine was on fire with the news that a couple thousand pounds of marijuana was at play. Those guys kept tabs on what law enforcement was up to, day and night. He really wished he could get to his hidden gun. It was taped under the tiny kitchen sink with about five hundred bricks of dope in front of it. For now he'd have to keep on looking like a dopey old man. It was beginning to get tiresome though. He knew that one way or another he'd be able to outwit Hammer. But a gang of bikers might just be beyond his abilities. The bikers were beginning to make him nervous. Hammer was jittery but Nathan didn't think he really understood how much danger he was in. If Dani didn't somehow intervene there was going to be two unmarked graves in the forest. And he really didn't want to spend eternity next to a dimwit like Hammer.

Nathan noticed the next biker picked them up just on the outskirts of Brookings. That was fast. And this time the biker hung back, keeping several RVs between them. Hammer was rotating his eyes from the front windshield to the side mirrors enough to satisfy even the most stringent defensive driving instructor. Still, Hammer didn't seem to notice that the biker behind them had missed two golden opportunities to pass the slow moving RVs in front of him. The biker wasn't interested in making good time.

"I wonder when they're going to jump you." Again Nathan was pleased with the way Hammer jerked at the sound of his voice.

"No one's going to jump me, Professor. If they do, what say I use you as a human shield? How would you like that, you old windbag?"

"Don't count on me stopping a bullet for you, Hammer. Chances are it will go right through me and end up in you. Bang. Bang. You'll be just as dead as I am. Here lies poor, poor Hammer. The bikers shot him and out he bled. Roll a joint my friends for poor, poor dumb Hammer. Tell me Hammer, how come you got stuck with the dangerous part of the job? Where's Dwight? Sounds like the master planner is keeping his hands nice and clean."

"*Shut the fuck up.*"

Nathan smiled and started humming. It was vaguely like "Man of Constant Sorrows", but since Nathan couldn't carry a tune it wasn't clear that Hammer got it.

About fifteen miles north of Brookings, Nathan watched as another biker joined the one behind them. They rode in tandem for a minute or so, then, with a couple of hand gestures, the first one roared ahead, easily passing the two RVs behind Nathan and Hammer. The bike didn't stop but sped on by, giving Hammer a small heart attack before he saw that it appeared not to be interested in him.

Nathan hoped Dani was able to pick up his text and track his phone. But the likelihood of being tracked diminished when Hammer suddenly took the Carpenterville exit and headed into the hilly areas east of Highway 101. Nathan had spent quite a bit of time in the area. It was one of the highest areas above the coast highways with terrific views of the coast. Carpenterville itself was considered a ghost town, though there wasn't much there anymore. The last Nathan knew, there was only one house left in the original location. When the coast highway was realigned back in the '30s or '40s, the town began losing what little population it had. Now, the Carpenterville highway meandered for about twenty miles before rejoining Highway 101 near Pistol River. And as Nathan knew, it was a lonely stretch that would make it ideal for the bikers to make their move. Hammer had to be one of the dumbest crooks he'd come across in a long time.

"So, Hammer. Where're we headed? One of these deserted cabins up beyond Carpenterville?"

"Getting nervous, old man? Thinking about when I tie you up and leave you in the woods for some big ole' bear? The thing about bears, they start eating you whether you're dead or not. Cougars at least will probably kill you before they start ripping your guts out." Hammer laughed in a particularly unpleasant way, like he was picturing the scene. He cracked another beer, his third in the last hour.

"As a betting man, I don't see it that way." Nathan made an

exaggerated glance at Hammer's side mirror. "Odds are, I'll just get shot in the crossfire. Hell, they may even let me go. I'm not the one stupid enough to sell drugs in their territory."

Hammer laughed, "Not this time old man. Ain't no one coming after me now. It was you just messing with my head." He took a long look out, but apparently didn't see the biker who was hugging the back of Iowa's truck.

"Oh they're there Hammer. Just hanging to the back of Iowa's bumper. Call him."

Hammer drove another half mile, ducking his head back and forth and not seeing anything.

"Shit." He picked up his phone and called the Iowa driver. The call didn't go through, they'd lost cell phone service. He held the phone out the window hoping to pick up a signal. The RV was weaving slightly as Hammer drove one handed with most of his attention on what was behind him. He looked up just in time to see a six-point buck crossing the road in front of him. He dropped the phone and swerved so suddenly that he put the RV in a skid. They were going sideways down the road, then he injudiciously applied the brakes and caused the RV to spin about and end up facing the opposite way. The engine died and the last sound was the Iowa driver as his truck laid a solid line of black rubber on the road. It managed to stop, just clipping the rear corner of the RV like a soft kiss. Behind him a motorcycle lay on the side of the road. The rider was half in the ditch and not moving.

Nathan came to rest amid a tumbled stack of marijuana

bricks. A somewhat soft landing for which he was grateful. He struggled back to his seat and looked out the window. Hammer was moaning softly, twisted half in his seat. A bloody cut above his eye from hitting the steering wheel was streaking his face and blinding him. Nathan raised his hands above his head and brought them down in one swift hard motion. Sitting, unable to stand, he didn't have the momentum to break the tape in one try. He did it again and suddenly his hands were free. He leaned over the driver's seat and ran his hand along the floorboards searching for the gun. Hammer shifted, beginning a long string of curses. Nathan looked out the windshield to see what the Iowa driver was doing. The man had climbed out of his truck and walked over to the spilled bike rider. He just stood there looking down on the crumpled body. Nathan had the impression that the bike rider was going to leave the scene in a black body bag. He cursed to himself. Hammer was becoming more aware, and Nathan still couldn't lay his hands on the damn gun. He shoved Hammer against the driver's door and climbed into the front passenger seat. He had the door open and one leg out when he heard the metal slide of the gun and now there was a bullet in the chamber.

"Not so fast, Professor."

Nathan considered dropping down outside the door and legging it into the thick trees just ten feet away. But, at this distance, he realized that Hammer wasn't likely to miss. He brought his leg back into the truck and closed the door. He turned and found the gun about a foot from his face. Hammer was wiping the blood from his eyes, smearing a mask of red over his face. He had a nasty grin on his face.

"I'm almost sorry you did that. This has been one shitty day and I wouldn't mind taking my frustrations out on your worthless pointy head." Hammer took a deep breath and turned with a start to find the Iowa driver at his window looking on.

"*Jesus.*" Hammer jerked back from the window. "The bike rider, is he dead?"

"Looks that way. I think we should go."

"Brilliant idea, Sherlock. It ain't far." Hammer started the RV. "You stay put, Professor. You still have a date with that ole' bear." He got the RV turned around and drove quickly down the road.

Nathan wasn't sure if he was still in the frying pan or now in the fire. Neither place looked propitious to him. He wished he'd had enough time to check his phone to see if there was service. Not likely in these coastal hills. Dani was going to have a hard time tracing him. Another few miles and Hammer slowed, then turned right onto Bull Gulch Road. There was a dead end sign at the intersection. There was only going to be one way out now.

They drove in silence, the road undulated lazily, heading into the Siskiyou National Forest. If there were houses or cabins, you couldn't see them from the road. Hammer kept an eye on the odometer; he was tracking the miles to the turnoff. He slowed the RV down to about ten miles an hour and kept his eyes peeled to the left. He spotted the barely trammeled track and turned the RV onto a rutted dirt drive, the green undergrowth of salal and manzanita encroaching on the road. They bumped along for about half a mile and then the way opened to a small meadow. There was an old log cabin sitting by a dry creek bed. The cedar shingles were buried under pine needles and forest duff, and the roof sagged as it sloped away from the stone chimney. The cabin looked abandoned and dismal.

Hammer parked the RV in front of the cabin and Iowa pulled his alongside. Hammer sat for a moment, thinking. His primary problem was the Professor. He needed to secure him while he and the driver unloaded the RV. The Iowa driver stood staring at the dilapidated cabin.

"You all don't actually stay in this dump, do you?" His flat nasal voice was full of Iowa distaste of dirt and disorder.

"Have I told you lately what a pussy you are? Go inside and find me some rope or something so I can tie the Professor up so he won't be underfoot."

"You're crazy. I ain't going in there. God knows what's inside." Iowa gave Nathan a considering look and added, "Why the hell tie him up? He looks strong enough to me. Make him help us."

Hammer grunted, his tone saying how much he didn't like that Iowa had come up with a good idea instead of him. He waved the gun at Nathan and Nathan climbed out slowly.

The next two hours were monotonously spent handing one brick of marijuana to another in a daisy chain of motion. And Nathan was stuck in the middle. At all times Hammer or Iowa had an eye on him.

"That's it. Last toke over the line." Hammer chuckled at his own joke.

"I only counted seventeen hundred eighty-nine bricks."

"We told you we were light. No one's trying to cheat you, Iowa."

"Not saying that. Just wanted to be clear about the money." Iowa jumped from the back of his truck and started to close the doors.

"Hold on. Why don't you get the money before you close it up? Like you said, we want to be clear about the money." Hammer followed him around to the side of the truck; Iowa dropped down to the ground and rolled under it. Hammer stooped down to watch where the money had been hidden in a metal container latched to the bottom of the truck.

Nathan took advantage of Hammer's momentary lack of attention and stepped into the RV. He went to the sink and groped underneath. If he could get the gun, he could start evening the odds. Just as his hand felt the tape, he heard Hammer behind him.

"What'ya doing, Professor?"

Nathan didn't turn. He reached for a small drawer at the side of the sink and pulled out a vial of pills.

"Just getting an ibuprofen. My back's killing me." Still

without looking at Hammer he opened the small refrigerator and pulled out a bottle of water. The cold water tasted good and he wasn't lying about needing the pain meds.

"Don't be selfish, Professor, toss the bottle here."

Nathan turned and threw the bottle toward Hammer, who had to reach high to grab it. Hammer poured about four pills out of the bottle and reached into his cooler again for another beer. The sweat from working had washed the blood from his face, and his green tee-shirt was splotched red where he'd wiped his face on it.

"Throw that roll of paper towels over to me." Hammer tore off a bunch of towels and dipped them in the ice and water in his cooler. He rubbed his face and neck with a look of exhausted satisfaction.

Nathan could hear the other truck back away and start down the dirt road. One less asshole to deal with. Now the question was, what did Hammer really have planned for him?

"Come on out. I have something to show you." Hammer waved the Glock and Nathan did what he said. The Glock still gave Hammer a superior edge. Nathan had no desire to have a shootout. His little Sig Sauer, if he could get his hands on it, was for when Hammer let his guard down. A couple more beers should do the trick.

Out of the RV, Nathan could no longer see the sun. It had dropped behind the trees to the west and the air was already getting a slight chill. Hammer had him walk around the side of the cabin to where a rusty old bicycle leaned against the wall. Hammer paused and picked up an old bicycle chain that was lying in the grass. For a moment, Nathan wondered if he should have tried to get a drop on Hammer. He had an image flash briefly through his mind of kneeling in the dirt behind the cabin and Hammer shooting him in the head. He hadn't figured Hammer as a stone cold killer. He seemed more of a blowhard, not an executioner. But maybe his radar for that kind of thing was as rusty as his other former skills.

Behind the cabin was a small wooden outhouse and that was where Hammer was guiding him. Nathan didn't think it was because Hammer was being thoughtful.

"Open it. See, nice and cozy. Time for you to take a little nap with the spiders while I get me some rest too."

Hammer wasn't joking about the spiders. Nathan waved down the webs in the doorway and looked at the splintery wooden shithole. He edged in around the door and turned in time to see the broad grin on Hammer's face as he reached in to close the door. He heard the clink of the chain. The door rattled as Hammer fastened it closed with the old bicycle chain. He was laughing while he did it. It was dark in the outhouse and only a small opening in the roof let any light in. It had a dank musty smell and the whole structure seemed rotten. He lifted a foot and gave the seat a gentle nudge. It seemed sturdy enough. It had a lid, which he lowered and gingerly sat on. Well, this wasn't what he expected. His stomach growled loudly and he realized he'd had nothing to eat since Claudie's delicious salmon. He thought about her again.

If he got out of this he was going to try to change her view of him as a fussy old bookstore owner. He had a lot of time to think about this. He heard Hammer climb into the RV and then a loud thud. There was a small crack toward the top of the door and he stood on tiptoe and looked out. He couldn't see the RV but he picked up on a flashlight through the window of the cabin. It was moving around like Hammer was exploring. The light stopped and fixed on the stone fireplace. Nathan could see Hammer walk in front of the light, bent over like he was dragging something. A few minutes later there was a loud susurration of beating wings and Nathan could see flickering shapes erupt out of the chimney. Bats. What was Hammer up to?

Half an hour later, Hammer was sprawled out on the bed with a half empty bottle of beer and a freshly rolled joint. Ten minutes later he was snoring. The roach dropped on the blanket, but before it could scorch it, the beer bottle tilted out of Hammer's hand and put it out. If the windows had been open, Nathan would have heard the snores.

Nathan pulled his phone out and turned it on. He used the flashlight to inspect his temporary quarters. At least, he hoped they'd be temporary. The door and walls were cedar, weathered but not rotten. There wasn't room for a running start at the door. He braced a foot against the door and shoved it. It didn't give at all. The door was mounted on the inside. He was pushing against the frame and it was firm. He looked up and the roof looked vulnerable, but when he stood on the toilet seat he heard a disconcerting crack and he hopped down. Drowning in a shithole was not how he wanted to depart this universe. He sat and noticed his phone had picked up a text from his niece; he probably caught a signal in Brookings. He read it and smiled. The text message was about the bungee jumping again. Ellie was a very persistent woman. Eric and his friends were going to jump off the Thomas Creek Bridge north of Brookings. It was the highest bridge in Oregon and Ellie was still imploring him to join them. It didn't look like that was in the cards. It was completely dark now, and it was apparent he was going to spend the night here. When he got out, he was going to repay Hammer, somehow, someway. It wasn't going to be pleasant, for Hammer that is. Then it came to him. The hinges. He shined the light and he smiled. Rusted old screws with slotted screw heads. He began searching his pockets. He had a couple of dimes. He had his work cut out for him.

Chapter Eleven

Thursday early afternoon

Dwight drove back to his house and parked the Malibu in the garage. God, his head still hurt from the hangover, and he was starving. He looked like shit. He was still in the same clothes he'd been wearing since the heist. He splashed cold water on his face and then went back to the living room. Sprocket was sprawled on the couch, dead to the world. He fought the urge to send him on his way to loser hell. Dwight confined himself to a hard swat as he passed Sprocket on the way to the kitchen.

Sprocket flailed his arms and ended up rolling off the couch. "What the fuck …" He wiped his mouth, smearing drool across his bristly cheek. "What's wrong with you, Dwight? Why are you always messing with me?"

"When I finally mess with you, Spock, you will know exactly why I'm doing it. I'm going over to the diner and grab something to eat."

"Why don't I get to have breakfast?" He stood up and hitched his pants up. "And stop calling me Spock. I don't call you names. I could too. I remember when the other cousins called you 'tighty whitey'. You didn't like it none."

"It hardly scarred me for life, *Sprocket*. I wear big boy pants now, and I'm the one going to the diner because I'm not the one suspected of ripping off Hoyt's mother-in-law's dope. Got that through your numbskull?"

"Yeah, well …" Sprocket muttered and went into the bathroom. He came back out with a toothbrush in his mouth. "Where's the fucking dog? If you're so smart, how come you don't have the dog?"

"Cause there's like a brigade of commandos there waving guns. Mindy Lou found that truck in nothing flat. She must have put some kind of tracker on it. Don't worry, I know where the dog is."

"Where?" It came out more like "air" since the toothbrush was still dangling from his mouth.

"The old lady has it. It looked like her car broke down and Hoyt was poking around under the hood. Hey! Is that my toothbrush?"

Sprocket went back to the bathroom and shut the door.

"Jesus." Dwight checked his cell phone to see if there were any messages from Hammer and was dismayed when he found no new messages, just the three voicemail messages from earlier. Christ, these two were killing him. He poured a large glass of water and sat at the table, trying to make a plan. Sprocket came out and opened the refrigerator. There was nothing but beer inside so he shut it and went into the living room and turned on the TV. Dwight sighed, "We need to drive over to Hoyt's and see what's up with her and her car. If she's headed out of town I need to know where she's going. We got to get that damn dog."

"Damn, she stole the dog. Why can't we just go up to her and take it?"

"Cause I don't think you should be calling attention to yourself just now. If they get prints off the delivery truck they're going to come looking for Hammer, and trust me, they'll be looking at you next."

"Hammer said he wiped it down."

"I don't trust Hammer to wipe his ass. I could bet a million dollars that he missed something."

"Want me to try to sweet talk Aileen into giving me my truck back? Maybe she's in a better mood now. Had time to think it through."

"Have at it, lover boy. But personally I don't think your sweet Aileen *has* any better moods. I think she's stuck in a pissing war with us, and isn't inclined to alter her course of action."

Sprocket gave a truculent grunt and went outside. Dwight re-listened to the voicemails starting with the oldest. The first one was before Hammer had made it to Crescent City and was one long grumble about how long it was taking him and how tired and hungry he was. In the second one he was noticeably less whiney; he'd had a big lunch at a roadside diner. He started rhapsodizing about the giant trees along the highway. Dwight cut the message off. He sure as hell didn't want to listen to a travelogue. Fucking nitwits.

The third message was left about an hour ago while he was driving up Highway 101. Hammer was complaining about traffic and how the other drivers kept slowing down to look at the scenery. It ended with Hammer saying, "Oh fuck. It's the one-eyed truck. It's behind me. How the hell did those guys ..." There was a long gap before Hammer started talking again. He was calmer now, but still edgy. That was the last message.

Now what? Dwight didn't like that there were no new messages. He selected the last message and listened again. Hammer's voice sounded panicky. He was convinced that the pick-up behind him was the same one from Mugginsville. It had a right headlight out like the other one, and Hammer could see two big guys in the front seat. He thought he could see a rifle in the rear window. There was a small town coming up and he was going to stop at a drive-in or something and see if they drove on by. That was it. Fuck.

Dwight punched Hammer's number in, but it went straight

to voicemail. He cursed and ended the call. He took a couple of deep breaths. Cell phone coverage was lousy down in that coastal area. Probably Hammer was just in a dead zone. Dwight's mind stumbled over that phrase, dead zone. He shook his head. *Don't lose your cool, man.* He tried the other driver's number but the same thing happened, it went directly to voicemail. Okay, they were in a dead zone. Or maybe they had already completed the transaction and were each on their way home. Hammer could already be at the cabin outside Pistol River. With all that lovely money. Hammer was just freaking out about the guys in the truck. There wasn't any way they could have followed him to Crescent City. It didn't make sense. He sent a text asking for an update.

Dwight hauled himself up and found the keys to his old VW bus. He kicked Sprocket's foot as he passed through the living room.

"Come on. We don't want to lose the old lady."

Thursday late afternoon

Claudie caught the first raindrops about ten miles outside Merlin as she drove toward the Rogue River. She was glad that she was driving the Subaru instead of her old BMW, since the Bear Creek Road proved to be one of the most narrow, crooked roads she'd ever driven. It was perhaps a mistake to take the direct route to Gold Beach. Her alternative would have been to drop down into California toward Crescent City and then pick up the coast highway. It would have added over a hundred miles and she didn't want to take the extra time. A sense of urgency was beginning to build inside of her. It wasn't going to go away until she knew for certain that Nathan was safe, even if it turned out he was a bit of a skunk.

The rain cut visibility and when she stopped at a viewpoint, she could tell the temperature had dropped at least ten degrees since Merlin. It took her nearly an hour to go the short distance from Merlin to Galice. In Galice, she stopped at the quaint country store and went in to see if they had a better map than her Oregon highway map. When she told the man behind the counter where she was headed, he asked her what she was driving. He seemed satisfied when he found out that it was a four-wheel drive. He suggested she stop at the Agness store and ask about road conditions. Sometimes rockslides blocked the road. Between Merlin and Agness the road was sometimes just one lane. The section of the road that was dirt and gravel would be challenging in the rain. She thanked him, she wasn't too worried; she had taken a winter driving class the previous January and had become quite proficient handling a vehicle when it went into a skid or spin. She paid for her drink.

"That your car, lady?"

"Huh?" She became aware that a car alarm was sounding outside the store. She came out of the store and sure enough the Subaru was blaring an alarm and the parking lights were blinking. She pressed the key fob and it became quiet again.

Who would have thought that Hoyt would have installed a car alarm on the junker? She noticed a white VW van that had parked down a few spaces from her; she had read that Volkswagen was going to start producing the vans again. Personally, she thought it was nostalgia run amok. She had no fond memories of a vehicle that broke down as often as the VW van did. A man was sitting inside with his head buried in a large map. She wasn't the only one without GPS.

She opened her door and for a puzzled moment couldn't see the dog. She looked in the back and the seat was empty, but sitting on the floor was a trembling Border Collie.

"Oh, you poor baby. Did the alarm scare you? Come up here, you big doofus, nothing's going to get you." He blinked at her with his large brown eyes and then, like slow moving lava, oozed into the passenger seat. He briefly looked out the window at the white van and then shifted so he was facing her. She gave him a couple of pats, which he interpreted as an invitation for slobbery kisses. She informed him they weren't necessary.

The next few miles would probably be the most difficult. After that, it sounded like a breeze. She was looking forward to views of the mountains and the Rogue River. Although sun would have been nicer, she still liked the mountains in the misty Pacific Northwest rains. She pulled her car out; the rain was coming down harder now and she made sure her lights were on. She didn't notice the white van pulling onto the road behind her. The van didn't bother with lights and was almost invisible in the rain and against the grey pavement.

"What the hell, Sprocket? Why didn't you just break the damn window and grab the dog?" Dwight looked with disgust at Sprocket as he tried to climb into the passenger seat. He was soaked and a dull scowl covered his face.

"I don't know, the fucking alarm. It surprised me and I could see the lady coming out the door. Turn on the heat, Dwight, I'm freezing."

"It is on. This is a piece of shit VW van, Sprocket. It's cold in winter and hot in summer. You want comfort, buy Japanese, not German."

"Sure. You know what? When I get my cut, I'll buy Aileen one of those Mercedes and she'll stop thinking I'm such a loser."

"Hope springs eternal. God, what is this woman thinking? This has to be one of the worst piece of shit roads in the State of Oregon and she's driving it in Hoyt's crappy Subaru."

"Bet it handles better than your piece of shit."

Dwight ignored this, although it rankled. His mother had left him this particular piece of shit. She told him once that she had conceived him in the back. Of course she'd remember that but not exactly who she'd done the deed with. Knowing his mother's low standards, he figured his father was probably just some roadie for an also ran, second bill punk band.

He didn't worry about hanging back from the Subaru. The

old lady wouldn't suspect that she was being followed and he wanted to stay close while he tried to figure out what to do. He needed to think fast. This section to Agness would be the best stretch to try to pull something. They were going to have to take the direct approach and force her off the road. He didn't have time to diddle around all the way to Gold Beach. The road ahead narrowed down to one lane that had occasional turnouts to let opposite traffic go by. It gave him a bright idea. He'd come up fast and make her pull into one of the turn outs and then park beside her and force her to hand over the dog. It should scare the pants off her to be blocked in and one thing Sprocket could do right is look scary. Dwight was quite proud of his plan. Couldn't fail. He explained it to Sprocket and even he couldn't see a flaw in it.

First thing is, he turned on his lights and pulled right up to the Subaru's bumper. He flashed his lights for good measure. And damn if she didn't pull over into the next turnout. He drove the van right up to her door and parked it.

"You're on, Sprocket. Be convincing."

"I can't." Sprocket opened his door a crack but that was all he could. Dwight had parked the van too close to the Subaru for him to get out.

"Jesus frigging Christ." Dwight hopped out of his side.

Sprocket was still looking down into the old lady's quizzical eyes. She didn't look afraid; she looked pissed.

"Sprocket, you dumb fuck. Get out of the van." Sprocket turned and finally started trying to heft himself over the gearshift and into the driver's seat. He couldn't fit. Dwight was a much narrower person than he was. Dwight reached in and made the seat go back and Sprocket nearly did a face plant on the seat. Righting himself, he finally climbed out and went around to the Subaru.

The old lady watched him through the windshield. Sprocket couldn't see the dog. He went to the passenger side and looked in. No dog, no dog in the back seat either. Where the hell did he go? Ah, Sprocket caught sight of a tip of white tail on the floor behind the driver. He tried the door but it was locked. He motioned to the old lady to open it but she shook her head. Her car was still running but she had nowhere to go.

"Open the door, you old bat. I want my dog." He thought he was being reasonable. The lady didn't seem to agree. He thought about using his elbow to smash the window but remembered the time he did that in high school. Broke his elbow in three spots. Plus, everyone knew it was him that had broken into the principal's car. He looked down for a rock but didn't see anything large enough. He went back to the van where Dwight was trying to watch without the old lady seeing him.

"I need a tire iron or something."

Dwight groaned and reached under the driver's seat. He came up with a hammer, "Will this do?"

Sprocket took it without a word and went back to the Subaru. Just as he was swinging back with the hammer, he heard a sudden roar of motorcycle engines. He looked up to see three motorcycles stopped in front of the VW van. The van was blocking the road. The bikers looked big and real mean. There was a chick sitting behind one of them but she looked as scary as the tattooed men. She was staring straight at him (and his arm with the hammer raised over his head). The old lady started to honk her horn.

The lead biker had a chain out now and was twirling it around in the air. With a thunderous crunch it landed on the VW headlights and shards of glass tinkled to the road. Sprocket could hear Dwight screaming and then the van door slam shut. The van roared to life and started to back up faster as the bikes followed, the sound of the menacing engines filled the air. The way was suddenly clear for the Subaru and the old lady gunned it forward. The last Sprocket saw of it the old lady had rolled her window down and was flipping him off. He dropped the hammer and started walking back toward Merlin. Dwight would eventually come back for him. He was sure of it. He checked his phone to see if Aileen had returned his call. No message. He sighed. The rain was cold and he had a long walk in front of him. Fucking old lady. She was going to get hers for stealing his dog.

Dwight didn't get scared until the bikers picked up speed and it was all he could do to make it around the last curve and not end up down in the ravine. This went on for almost a mile. Dwight wanted to shoot the fuckers but he couldn't take his eyes off his rear view mirrors. Besides, he didn't have a gun.

Finally he could see a viewpoint coming up behind him and he angled the van to slide into the pull off. The bikers sailed on by, horns blaring a giant "fuck you" to him as they disappeared around the next bend. He sat there with his hands on the wheel. Every time he lifted them, the trembling was so disturbing that he clutched the steering wheel again. His whole body was drenched in a rank cold sweat. While he sat, letting his body attempt normality again, he began to think about his goals in life. What was it that he wanted out of life? Money. The marijuana in Sprocket's truck represented a lot of money but did he really need it? By now, Hammer should be sitting on a much bigger pile of money at the cabin. It was like the bird in the hand and why the fuck did he need to mess around with Sprocket's shit? Let him get the truck back from his demented ex-girlfriend and he could have the marijuana as his cut. Dwight was done with the moronic shithead.

He made a laborious six-point U-turn to head back to Merlin. He'd dump the stupid van, get his Malibu, and then take Highway 199 the long way to the cabin. Sprocket could just fend for himself. That old broad was not going to let the dog go without a fight, and she looked like she could outwit his lump of a cousin without breaking a sweat.

If Sprocket had ever paid attention when his father was teaching him how to track and hunt, he'd have noticed the churned up gravel on the viewpoint. But he trudged on by. It was beginning to occur to him that Dwight wasn't coming back for him. It was possible that the bikers had ridden his bumper till he crashed the van. Dwight could be hurt or in trouble. It was a possibility for sure. But Sprocket's life experience told him that once again he was being screwed. His dreams of a secure future, maybe a little house in eastern Oregon where no one knew him, a life with Aileen, maybe a couple of kids, even the damn dog, those dreams were as cold and soggy as the drizzle that had now penetrated through every stitch of his clothing. Walking in wet jeans was like wading through Jello. It took him a couple of hours to make it back to Galice.

He went into the store and bought a cup of hot coffee. He tried calling Dwight but it went straight to voicemail. He left a message that embarrassed him, it sounded so needy. What the hell. He tried Aileen again and was surprised when she answered on the second ring.

"Aileen? This is Sprocket."

"Where's Jasper Sprocket?"

"Ummm, you see, I think he's headed to Gold Beach. Some old lady has him and ..."

"What the hell? Why is some old lady driving my dog to the beach for god's sake?"

"I don't really know. I tried to get him from her but she wasn't very cooperative. I think I really need you to help out here. Maybe you could reason with her."

"Yeah, reason isn't exactly your strong point is it?" There was a long silence, and then, "Okay. I was planning on going to Pistol River for the Biker rally anyway. Oleg's playing a couple of gigs there. I could meet you someplace and we could look around Gold Beach for Jasper and your old lady."

"That would be great, honey. Uhh, there's one thing. I don't have a ride. I need you to pick me up in Galice."

"In Galice? How the hell did you get out there?"

"Long story. You pick me up and I can tell you all about it."

Aileen huffed into the phone and Sprocket held his breath. "Okay, where?"

"At the Galice Country Store."

"Fine, I can be there in about an hour."

"Uhh, honey? Do you still have that …" Sprocket looked up to see the storeowner looking at him, "… cargo we talked about?"

She hesitated, "Oh, yeah. It's still under that shit motorcycle of Hammer's. I don't even want to touch it. If I get stopped it won't be my DNA all over it."

"Good, good. I'll see you in about an hour."

Sprocket disconnected and went and got a shopping basket. He was starved, and Aileen didn't like him eating in the truck. It was his truck, true, but she hated the smell of jerky and everything else he liked to eat. He needed not to irritate her. In fact, he was hoping that if he played his cards right, he might come out of this a hero. He'd have to make rescuing Jasper into something like an Avenger would do. He couldn't think which one, but some super hero, one who would make her forget about that dweeb Oleg and his stupid guitar.

An hour later, Sprocket opened the pick-up door and

climbed in next to Aileen. Boy, she was looking good. All sparkly. He breathed in the smell of her hair. He liked the kiwi-scented stuff she used. He missed that.

"Jeeze, Sprocket, you're soaked. What the hell happened?"

"The VW broke down. I had to walk a couple of miles in the rain. Can we turn the heat up?"

"Christ, no, you smell like a wet dog already. Now, do you want to tell me what this is all about? I just heard on the radio the co-op's grass got stolen. Now I'm driving your pick-up and I find a bunch of marijuana in the truck bed and I hate to think you had anything to do with that."

"Not me. My cousin said he was working on a business deal and needed my help. He wanted me to deliver some stuff for him."

"Sprocket, you're such a dope. Who is this cousin? He's got you running around with a boatload of stolen grass in your truck. It's real suspicious, don't you think?"

"No. First of all, I was camping Wednesday night. That's when Jasper went missing. Me and Hammer were going to go fishing and I forgot my tent, see. So that's why I came home. You saw me at my place, had nothing to do with that."

"Which is it? Camping or delivering some 'stuff'. Where'd the dope come from?"

Sprocket screwed up his face. The questions were coming too fast. "It's Dwight's. He bought some to take back to ahh … wherever he lives."

"Dwight's your cousin? The one I talked to this morning?"

Sprocket nodded. He wasn't cold anymore. He felt a hot flush throughout his body and he started to sweat. He hoped he wasn't getting a fever.

"How come you don't know where he lives?"

"He never told me. That way I couldn't, uhh, tell the wrong people."

"Damn, Sprocket. You've got yourself in so much shit. I should just kick you out right now. You aren't lying about that old lady and Jasper, are you? If you are, I'll shoot you myself."

"No, I'm not. She stole your dog at the campsite. You take me to Gold Beach and I can point her out to you, I swear." Things were getting really confusing for Sprocket. He needed Aileen to get him away from here. Maybe he'd let Dwight and Hammer split the money. He could take off with the stuff in back. He could live a long time on it, just deal out a few bags here and there. Just get as far away as he could. Now if he could just convince Aileen that she'd be better off with him instead of running after some loser guitar player, Oleg. What a stupid name. He looked like a doofus too. And his guitar playing was shit. Sprocket looked at Aileen. She was so pretty. He needed to find and save that dog. Make her appreciate him. Get a little payback on that stupid old lady.

Chapter Twelve

laudie's heart didn't stop racing till she was parked in front of the Agness store. Buddy was still cowering on the floor in the back. She checked her cell phone. Still no signal, so she got out, made sure she locked the car, and went into the store. It was empty but she could smell something heavenly and in a few seconds an older woman came out from the back carrying a large pan of what turned out to be blueberry crisp. Claudie asked if there was a pay phone and the woman directed her to where there was one down the street. Claudie started to leave. Then, ensnared by the scent of blueberries and cinnamon, she decided an infusion of sugar was what her nervous system needed.

Outside she looked for any sign of the van and then went to find the phone. She left a message for the sheriff about her run in with the van and Sprocket. She left out the part about the dog. She wasn't a dognapper; she was a rescuer. She regretted she hadn't been cool and collected enough to get the van's license plate number. But, under the circumstances, she was proud she had managed to drive fifty miles an hour on the twisty narrow road without spinning out on the gravel. Last winter's training had kicked in and she had kept the car on the road. The next section heading into Gold Beach was two lanes and paved all the way. She'd have to come back another time to enjoy the views. She intended to make good time to put some distance between her and that crazy man.

The drive gave her plenty of time to speculate about Sprocket and his pursuit of the dog. He hadn't struck her as being emotionally attached to the dog and by all appearances Buddy wasn't too fond of him. And if Sprocket was running around looking for the dog, where was Mindy Lou's marijuana? Even more important, where was Nathan and his RV?

Claudie finally picked up a cell phone signal as she dropped down into Gold Beach. She drove south over the bridge where the Rogue River spilled out to the sea under a gunmetal gray sky. She was hungry and needed a place to sit, make some calls, and maybe come up with a plan. Driving around blindly looking for Nathan would be stupid and a waste of time. She found a little place called Barnacle Bistro and parked the car. Buddy sat up and looked around then yawned widely and settled down again. She'd need to walk him and find some better food for him besides the few bites of blueberry crisp she had shared. Outside the car the rain was misty and she took some deep breaths of the sea air. The Bistro was mostly empty. It was between lunch and dinner, but the warm enticing smell of fish and chips set her stomach growling. She sat at one of the small wooden tables and a waitress was there in an instant with a menu and a glass of water. She looked the menu over, decided to pass on the Drunken Hog Fries, and ordered the fish and chips with a glass of white wine. When her food came, she practically inhaled the delicious fish and chips. The white wine was drinkable but nothing to get excited about. She didn't care. It helped settle her nerves.

She went up to the cash register to pay and while she waited for the waitress to come over, she looked at the small billboard advertising local events. The fall harvest festival was coming up in a couple of weeks. The community theater's last summer performance of *The King and I* had taken place on Labor Day weekend. Dang, she missed that. The waitress gave her change and she was almost out the door when it struck her. Nathan had said his brother had performed in community theater, but it hadn't been *The King and I*. She went back and looked at the flier again. There it was, "Gold Beach's Own King Plays the King of Siam". There could only be one. She scanned for the actor's name and found King Wesley in the boldest font. It had to be him.

She waved the waitress over, "Perhaps you can help me? I'm here for a wedding. My favorite nephew is getting married this weekend and I've lost the directions to the bride's house. Her last name is Wesley?"

"Oh, yeah. I heard Ellie was getting married. Everyone has heard about it. King's putting on this big extravaganza. Got the whole town buzzing to see what he's up to." She laughed and then took a piece of paper and started writing down the directions. "You basically go up hill till you get to the biggest house with the best view in town and you'll be there. Can't miss it. I'm not kidding. King tells everyone you can see it from the space station."

Claudie thanked her and went back to her car. She'd passed a pet store a couple blocks back, so she put Buddy on his rope leash and they walked back to it. She bought him a decent leash and collar and a good brand of dog food. Buddy was so friendly to the clerk that he got not one, but two treats. Claudie was beginning to see that Buddy knew how to ingratiate himself with people. On the way out she stopped and turned back. Poop bags. The downside of having a dog in a city, you had to pick up their poop. She took the food back to the car and put some in a dish. It was gone in thirty seconds. Then they took a stroll down to the ocean. There wasn't anybody walking on the beach so she took him off the leash and let him run in the surf for a bit. It wasn't till they were back at the car that she realized her mistake. The wet sandy dog hopped in the back and sat looking at her with happy brown eyes. Oh well, that's why they invented vacuums. She looked at the directions and headed up to what had to be the biggest frigging house on the southern Oregon coast.

It certainly looked like a place fit for a King. The driveway was short, but the circular parking in front of the house could handle a least a dozen cars. It was a grey stucco mansion. She could see two stories from the landward side, but coming up she had caught glimpses of the ocean facing side. She counted three levels with landscaped terraces sloping down to the edge of the property. In the front was a brick tower and on one corner was a turret. The windows were wood framed and huge and Claudie thought the maintenance must cost a fortune. The front door was massive and made out of some wood that Claudie didn't recognize. It was reddish and deeply grained and smack in the middle was a huge bronze knocker in the shape of a lion's head. The king of cats, of course.

She left Buddy in the car and went up to the door and lifted the knocker and let it drop. It was very loud. She could hear it echo inside the house, but there was no response. She looked for a doorbell but didn't see one. She tried again with the knocker but silence reigned. She looked around. There were two other cars parked out front. Someone had to be there. There was a path to the right that meandered through some landscaping and around to the side of the house. She looked over to her car; Buddy was watching her intently. Probably not a good idea to show up at the door with a sandy, wet dog.

She took the path and found a four-bay garage on that side

of the house. She almost turned around but she could hear people talking—arguing, in fact. She went a little farther and found a small patio set back a little from the garage front. The back door to the kitchen opened out to it. The door was wide open and she walked up to it and looked in. She would have stood admiring the huge kitchen if she wasn't immediately transfixed by the sight of two women having a tug of war over a bright yellow colander of steaming pasta. The older woman had golden hair, courtesy of her hairdresser, and was dressed in a fuchsia silk blouse over slim black pants. The younger woman had natural blonde hair and was dressed in jeans and a white tee-shirt. The young woman was winning and the older woman acceded defeat by letting go of the colander so suddenly that the contents flew up and over the shoulder of the young woman. She stooped and picked up the spaghetti and plopped it back into the yellow colander. They both noticed her at the same time and stood looking at her. The older woman appeared a little embarrassed but the younger one just put a string of spaghetti in her mouth and chewed. In the background Claudie could hear Aaron Copeland's "Appalachia" playing softly.

"I'm sorry, I didn't mean to intrude …" Claudie got no further.

"You're half an hour late, I told Betty …"

"Mother, please. Betty said she'd send someone after the lunch service. It's fine. Did Betty tell you what I need you to do?"

"No, actually I'm not ..."

"The whole thing is ridiculous. I don't know why you persist with this idiotic notion. What's Eric's family going to think? Their first impression of us is going to be we're some kind of nuts. Colanders and pasta bouquets. I think ..."

"You've made it clear what you think, Mother. Why don't you go have a martini and let this lady help me put this together? Hi, my name's Ellie, what's your name?"

"My name is Claudie and I'm not here to help you ..."

"See, I told you. No one wants to help you ruin your wedding."

"Vodka, Mother. Let me handle this. So tell me, Claudie, what do you have against the Pastafarian[2] faith?" The young woman tried to keep a stern look on her face but her brown eyes were twinkling.

Claudie couldn't help but laugh. "I've nothing against Pastafarianism. Up to this moment I didn't know it existed. I do confess that I don't eat much pasta. Tomato sauces give me heartburn and pasta goes straight to my hips."

"Oh, you poor thing. Well, first thing we need to do is enlighten you about the Church of the Flying Spaghetti Monster, and while I do that you can help me dye this pasta. I'm trying to get a nice turquoise color and I'm not succeeding. Any suggestions?"

Claudie walked over to the sink and looked down at a pile

2   Church of the Flying Spaghetti Monster does exist. Google it.

of sickly green pasta. On the counter were several empty bottles of green and blue food dye.

"It looks like you're using whole-wheat pasta. Have you tried doing it with regular pasta?"

"Oh, my god. That's it. Hold on." She picked up a smart-phone and started texting. "There, Daddy's still downtown, he'll pick up some boxes on his way home." Ellie paused and looked at Claudie; she seemed suddenly aware that she had no idea why Claudie was there. "If Betty didn't send you to help me, why are you here?"

"I'm looking for your uncle, Nathan. He isn't here by any chance?"

"No, the big poop. He was supposed to go bungee jump-ing with Eric this afternoon." She paused and her eyes got big, "Are you his new girlfriend? Mother, come back in here. Uncle Nathan's new girlfriend is here. He said he had a sur-prise for me and there you are."

The older woman came back into the kitchen holding a very large martini glass. "What are you talking about Ellie?" She eyed Claudie with a skeptical eye.

"Uncle Nathan said he was bringing a surprise and Claudie must be it. It's about time he got himself a girlfriend. Oh, my god. I wonder if Daddy knows?"

Claudie felt she was being examined under the microscope of the mother's disapproving eyes. And found wanting. Her camping wardrobe was not up to snuff for Mrs. King Wesley.

"Don't be ridiculous, Nathan wouldn't just pop a girlfriend

on us without telling us. Where is Nathan?" Mrs. Wesley directed the question to Claudie.

"That's why I'm here. I'm looking for Nathan. I'm a little worried about him."

"Worried about Nathan? Don't be silly. That man leads the most orderly life in existence. Nothing happens to him that he hasn't planned and analyzed from all conceivable angles. Why are you looking for him?"

How to phrase this? She should have planned what she was going to say before blundering into this crazy house.

"We were camping on Wednesday, and …"

"You were camping with Uncle Nathan? How cool."

"We weren't actually camping together. Not in the same campsite, just the same campground. We had dinner together and something kind of strange happened." The two women looked at her expectantly. She described what happened that night and the next morning when she found Nathan missing.

"I think maybe you're reading too much into it. Nathan has avoided getting entangled since Kay died. He probably didn't want to cause you any hurt feelings and left early." Mrs. Wesley's brittle smile revealed that causing hurt feelings was something she did not avoid.

"Mother, Uncle Nathan would never have left her in that campground with that man. Maybe that's why he's late. He hasn't returned any of my messages and I *know* that he really was looking forward to bungee jumping off the bridge."

"There's more to the story." Claudie told them about her

car being shot, the medical marijuana that was stolen, and the men who tried to break into her car and grab the dog.

"Unbelievable." Which summed up Mrs. Wesley's attitude.

"Incredible. Wait, where's the dog?"

"He's out in my car."

"Poor boy. Let's go get him. He must be a wreck." Ellie headed out the door and around to Claudie's car. Without asking, Ellie opened the back door and Buddy hopped out. He was so happy to see them that he went back and forth from one woman to the other for hugs and kisses. He milked it for all it was worth. It confirmed Claudie's opinion that the dog was a shameful slut for attention. Ellie took the leash and headed back to the kitchen but Mrs. Wesley was standing guard at the door.

"Not in the house. No. You don't know what parasites that dog has. I'm not spraying for fleas … Ellie! He's filthy." Mrs. Wesley stood helplessly as her daughter brought Buddy inside and then put a bowl of water down for him. Buddy was not dainty in his drinking and Mrs. Wesley watched in dismay as water splashed onto the wood plank floor. Claudie went to the sink and grabbed a couple of paper towels and wiped up after the dog.

"The first thing we should do is give this big boy a bath." Ellie examined Buddy's ears and held up his paws to inspect the length of his nails. "In fact, Buddy, you need a complete makeover. Come on."

"Ellie, for god's sake. Leave the dog alone. If what this

woman says is true, we need to contact the police. Put out an APB or something."

"You and Daddy can work on that. I've got to get this boy ready for a wedding."

Claudie looked at the distraught Mrs. Wesley and decided that washing the dog would be a good way to give Mrs. Wesley time to mull over the story.

"I'm calling your father."

"Great, come on Claudie. I want to hear more about you and Uncle Nathan."

An hour later, Claudie left Ellie blow-drying Buddy's hair. She was wet and had a fine layer of black dog hair coating her. She needed to find a place to stay and take a shower. She could hear voices in the kitchen and headed that way. The music had changed to "The Music Man". In the kitchen, she found Mrs. Wesley sitting at the breakfast nook table with an elderly couple. At the kitchen island a short bald man chopped bell peppers. He was singing, full throttle, "Marion the Librarian". This must be the King. Regal he wasn't, but the speed and enthusiasm with which he chopped those vegetables told Claudie that this was a man used to getting things done. He looked up at her and Mrs. Wesley turned to stare. Claudie was acutely aware of her bedraggled appearance.

"You must be Claudie, Nathan's friend?" He paused in his chopping and singing and gave her a look that was a little less censorious than his wife's.

'Yes. I'm … *really* sorry about barging in here while you're in the middle of getting ready for the wedding. I've just been worried about Nathan and I wanted to check to see if he'd driven here or if I was just imagining the whole thing."

"I don't think that Nathan would have gotten mixed in anything that's remotely dicey. He taught numbers and logic for thirty years. He observes humanity, he does not get his hands dirty with the gritty side of life." King began dicing an onion. "My sister always said the problem was that I was like the comic pages, open and easy to read. Nathan was more like one of those literary books, the ones you have to delve down deep to figure out. Well, I could never get into that philosophy mumbo jumbo." He tossed the diced onions in the bowl with the red peppers and wiped his hands on a towel.

"Daddy! Uncle Nathan is not some fusty old book. He's a lot more fun than you give him credit for. Claudie, what do you think of your puppy now?" Ellie led a shiny and fluffy looking Buddy into the kitchen. Claudie noted that Ellie still looked good. Somehow she had rid herself of Buddy's hair. Buddy came over for Claudie's approval and sat by her feet and looked directly at King.

"Claudie, I am forgetting my manners. Can I pour you a glass of wine?"

"That sounds lovely but I really need to find a motel and get cleaned up. I've got more hair on me than Buddy." Claudie couldn't help but notice the smirk on Mrs. Wesley's face. That was one person who would be glad to see the last of her bedraggled self. The old man and woman seemed to mirror Mrs. Wesley's assessment.

"Oh, no. Daddy, you can't let her go. Why can't she stay in the trailer? Eric's sister decided to stay with the other bridesmaids at the Seagull Inn." Ellie turned to Claudie, "You can take a shower in my room. Please. I want to hear more about you and Uncle Nathan."

"*Ellie.*" Mrs. Wesley pursed her lips and squinted daggers at her daughter.

King paused in chopping a zucchini, "You'd have trouble getting a room anyway, Claudie. There's an oceanic conference in Newport that spilled some visitors down here and of course all our relatives and friends have booked rooms. The dog makes it more difficult too. The trailer isn't fancy but you're welcome." He finished killing the zucchini and began to pry some garlic cloves apart.

"It's settled." Ellie popped a red pepper slice in her mouth.

"Really, I feel embarrassed enough, I couldn't …" What if Nathan showed up? What would he think about her taking up residence at his brother-in-law's house? And if Ellie started babbling about her claiming to be his girlfriend, it would be mortifying. Still, her skin was itching and the thought of searching from one end of town to the other for an empty room that would take a dog. It was exhausting to think about it.

"Go get your stuff and I'll show you upstairs."

Hell, it wouldn't be the first time she was mortified.

Sometimes it seemed like it was a constant theme in her life. She went out to the car and returned with her duffle bag. Mrs. Wesley's lip curled when she saw the old bag. She was beginning to not like Mrs. Wesley. In fact, annoying Mrs. W was becoming an attractive bonus to staying the night.

After her shower, Claudie put on a clean shirt and a pair of khaki pants that didn't look too ratty. Who packs nice clothes to tramp around in the woods? Ellie had put out the 'The Wiz', the King Supreme Grooming All-in-One contraption that had helped cement the Wesley fortune, but for the life of her she didn't know how to use it. She settled for wet hair. At least it was clean and combed. Downstairs the voices in the kitchen had increased in volume and variety. Around the kitchen island were three young men, all of whom could easily reach to the top shelf of the tallest cabinets. A useful feature in a man, Claudie thought, and there wasn't a bad looking guy in the mix. One of them had an arm around Ellie's shoulders; he must be the groom-to-be. He was describing how the high wind on the bridge gave the bungee jump an extra jolt of adrenaline. Ellie was listening with shining face and eyes, adoration oozing from every pore. Buddy was sitting at her feet, his head nestled into the palm of her hand and his eyes closed in bliss. Mrs. W was still sitting with the old couple at the breakfast nook table. She glanced at Claudie but went back to her conversation. King was at the wall oven pulling out a roasting pan that cradled a giant chunk of beef. He was wearing huge oven mitts on both hands and with his bald head and flushed face he looked a little like an overcooked lobster. The smell of the beef made Claudie's mouth water. She went over to him to see if she could help but he had it under control. He pointed to a bottle of California Cabernet and she gratefully poured herself a glass. The kids, they were all in their late twenties or so, were in a bubble of conversation that Claudie didn't feel like intruding on. She certainly wasn't going to join the coffee klatch at the breakfast nook so she drifted over to the back door and went out to the back patio.

"Claudie, I need to show you where you're staying tonight before it gets too dark." Ellie was in the doorway glimmering in a bride-to-be kind of way. "We parked the trailer over behind Gram and Gramp's little cottage. It has its own view and everything."

Claudie and Buddy followed her to the edge of the landscaped area. A small building that looked like a converted carriage house was tucked in by a long laurel hedge, and behind it a short gravel drive led to a dark red trailer. A horse trailer by the look of it.

"We fixed it up inside with a bed and table and stuff. And come see the adorable little patio."

Facing the ocean was an awning-covered patio with a cast iron table and two chairs. To the side in the waning sun was a cushioned lounge chair. Ellie flipped a switch and the area was outlined in tiny Christmas lights. It was rather cute.

"I think it's quite cozy inside. The bed is a double high air mattress and it's really comfortable."

The bed was covered with a floral comforter and several matching pillows. On the floor was a thin oriental carpet. An overstuffed chair in matching floral print sat by the door and a reading lamp on a small table completed the furnishings. It did look more comfortable than Claudie's tent and sleeping bag. Ellie turned the lamp on giving it all a soft warm glow.

"This is really nice. Eric's sister doesn't know what she's missing."

"Oh, she looked at it. And immediately called her girl-friends. She's kind of a priss. I thought since you go camping and all with Uncle Nathan you wouldn't mind. What do you think, Buddy?"

Buddy was sniffing at the edge of the bed and Claudie fervently hoped he wasn't going to lift a leg. Instead, he hopped on the bed and walked to the head and plopped down on the pillows.

"Uh uh, big boy. Not on the pillows. Down." Claudie pointed to the floor and the dog jumped down with not a sign of shame.

"You can drive your car down and park it right here by the patio. I'll meet you up at the house. Daddy's gone all out on dinner."

Claudie pulled her car up besides the trailer and sat for a moment looking out at the ocean. It was beautiful. Then she went back to the house where the beef was being sliced and a delicious dinner awaited.

She was put next to the older couple. Ollie and Alvin Wesley were King's parents and Nathan's former in-laws. Claudie in her various marriages had experienced a variety of in-laws. In all their diversity they shared one quality. They were all annoying. This pair was particularly intrusive. Ollie started the ball rolling.

"I didn't think that Nathan was ever going to get his pipes cleaned again. How long you known him?" Ollie took a sip of pink wine.

Claudie choked and almost spit a bit of beef across the table. That would have been unfortunate since Mrs. Wesley was sitting directly across from her. Her coughing fit elicited an elegant frown from Mrs. Wesley. Alvin had been tucking into his food and ignoring the women but he managed a brief pause to register a disapproving scowl in her direction.

Claudie took a large gulp of wine. "Nathan and I are really just friends. We haven't, ah …"

"Damn that boy. I loved my daughter Kay. I thought she did real good with Nathan. He took her to all these exotic places, and when she got sick he brought her home. My Alvin here, he never approved of all that gallivanting. He wanted Kay to stay home and come to dinner every Sunday like King." She finished her glass and looked over at Alvin. Alvin was busy with putting as much butter and salt on a baked potato as could possibly be accomplished. If he had ever worried about his cholesterol it was no longer a concern. Not that Claudie would fault him. In twenty years she wouldn't give a damn either. Claudie could see that Ollie was trying to keep Alvin from seeing her pour more wine. Claudie watched with a twinge of horror as she realized that Ollie wasn't drinking a blush wine, but a mixture of a very nice Chardonnay and an exceptional Washington Merlot. Mrs. Wesley was watching this too, a resigned expression on her face that shifted to a brittle smile when she caught Claudie looking at her.

"Why aren't you screwing him? You're a good enough looking woman, not exactly in the prime of life anymore. You got another boyfriend?"

"No, it's just …"

"What are you waiting for? You're not getting any younger, you use it or you lose it. Sex keeps you young. Look at Alvin and me." She took a long pull on her wine and started to cut her beef into very small bites. "Back when I was in the circus I used to have tons of admirers. I used to pick a new beau at each town we stopped at. More's the pity I got hurt in Medford and that's where I stopped. With Alvin."

"Ollie, what stories are you filling this woman with now?" Alvin had demolished the potato and was between courses.

"Just how we met when I came to town with the circus."

"Yeah, yeah. The fancy circus lady." Alvin leveled his squinty eyes at Claudie. "She was the ticket taker. That's all she was."

"That's not true. I was in training to work with the el-ephants. I was going to be in the next Portland show. Big

Harry promised me."

"Big Harry was a big bag of wind. He ran out of town without paying his people or his bills. That stupid elephant cost the city a couple tons of hay before the mayor got some other circus to take it."

"Mom, Dad. Can we not have the circus argument tonight? We don't want Ellie and Eric to see what marriage can deteriorate into." King stood behind his father with the platter of beef; he placed a large bloody chunk on his father's place, puckered his lips as he eyed Ollie's glass of pink wine, and then moved on round the table.

"I was just saying." Alvin started cutting his beef. He, too, favored small pieces.

Ollie made a face at him and looked around for the wine bottles but they had moved down to the other end of the table. She sighed heavily and drained her glass. She lost all interest in Claudie's love life for which Claudie was grateful. She could hear King at the other end of the table tell a long story about his honeymoon with Mrs. Wesley, who was clearly bored. She got up to clear plates and Claudie asked if she could help but Mrs. Wesley rejected her offer. Claudie decided that it was time to call it a night. She went down to the trailer and found Buddy stretched across the doorway waiting for her. She put his leash on and they went for a short walk.

She couldn't understand the Wesley family's attitude toward Nathan. It was like they believed that nothing ever bad or exciting ever happened to him. It was so unlike what she had come to realize about him. He had not chosen the easy safe path in life. Teaching abroad, especially in areas like the middle east, was not for the faint of heart. He returned home when his wife was dying and settled into the small town life of Sisters. But she wasn't so sure that was the full picture, or that the quiet life was all he had left in him.

Back in the trailer she undressed and got into bed. It was stuffy in the trailer so she opened the side windows to let a breeze in. Cool air wasn't all that drifted in through the windows. She was nestled under the covers, lights out, dog snug against her hip listening to the distant sound of the ocean when she heard the first squeaking. Coming in the window facing Alvin's and Ollie's little house was a rhythmic thudding that sounded like a headboard of a bed getting a serious workout. Low groans were layered on top and she tried so hard to tell herself that maybe one of the young people were out there getting it on. Then quite distinctly she heard Ollie say, "Oh, Alvin." Claudie leaped up in horror and shut the window closest to their little house. Alvin must have got his second wind because even with the window closed she could hear a short ten-second burst of thumping that would have made a rabbit proud. Claudie pulled her pillow over her head and curled up in a fetal position. She waited a minute to be sure they were done. Oh god, erase this from my memory. Please don't let me dream about this. Ever. But she knew, this could never be unheard. She felt like a kid who'd walked in on her parents. Scarred for life.

Thursday late afternoon

Dani glanced back to make sure the woman in the yellow Subaru had pulled away from the yahoo with the hammer. She grinned when she caught the woman's one-fingered salute to the yahoo. She turned back and watched as Zach and the other guys intimidated the shit out of the wimp in the van. Once they passed him the going was still slow. In the rain it was a lousy road for motorcycles. Finally they reached Merlin and she slugged Zach on the back and pointed to a little tavern.

"I need to pee." She shouted in his ear.

He swerved into the parking lot and the other bikers followed. No one was against taking a break out of the rain and a beer sounded good to all of them. There weren't very many customers in the small tavern and when the bikers came in several people hurriedly finished their beers and left. Dani headed to the women's restroom. It was a two staller and both of them were occupied by women who were carrying on a conversation in shrill, slightly boozy voices.

"Gawd, I would have loved to see Mindy Lou's face when she realized the dope was missing."

"Shit, I swear I heard her screech from a mile away." The women giggled and snorted.

"I still can't believe that Sprocket was the one. Seems a little too much for him to bite off and chew."

"Sprocket's just the fall guy. You know, like in the movies?

He's the one the smart one sets up to take the blame. Hammer has to be up to his neck in this."

"Hammer doesn't have a neck." They both laughed some more.

"And he ain't much brighter than Sprocket. It's dumb and dumber. There's someone else, mark my words."

"Someone said that there was some guy in an RV at the campground. Maybe he was the mastermind?"

"Shit, who knows?" First one woman flushed and then the other. They were startled to find Dani waiting by the sink. She had a couple of questions for them.

When they left, Dani checked her smartphone and read Nathan's text. He had somehow found his very own little gang of nasty boys. The tracker she'd put on Nathan's RV showed it sitting somewhere in the forest northeast of Brookings. Now she knew where she was headed; it was time to take a little side trip without any of her new biker friends.

She came out and sat by Zach. She leaned in and whispered about what she'd overheard, except she left out the RV part. He didn't notice that her hand on the table had swallowed up his keys. When she finished she stood, "I'm grabbing a smoke." Outside she headed straight to his bike and hopped on. She started to ease it away from the tavern when suddenly a beefy arm reached out and jerked her off the seat. She landed on her shoulder in the mud and felt a sharp stab of pain.

"You don't smoke." Zach climbed onto his bike and the other guys started theirs, all of them laughing at her as they tore out of the parking lot. Fuck.

She stood and knew immediately that something was wrong with her shoulder. She went back into the tavern and ordered a hot coffee. While she drank she weighed her options. They were limited by her injury. In the end she decided to head to Gold Beach, maybe someone at King Wesley's could help out. Maybe some handsome young groomsman looking for some excitement. Now, how to get to Gold Beach? She looked around the tavern; there were a few men at the bar who looked like they'd just got off work. One of them would do.

"Anybody here want to earn a couple hundred dollars?"

Chapter Thirteen

Late Thursday night

Hammer woke with a start. He was cold, it was black outside, and it was very still. He hated the forest. He didn't see the point of it, way too quiet. He rolled, fell off the bed, and found himself wedged in the narrow space between the bed and small dresser. His right arm was trapped beneath him and he couldn't get it positioned to help leverage himself up. He flailed his left hand around, there was nothing to grab onto. His cursing was muffled because his face was smashed into his arm. Eventually he wiggled out, like a snake backing out of its old skin, and sat on the floor breathing hard and cursing Dwight. Dwight should have been there by now. They could have divided up the cash, and he could have been on his way to Missouri by now. Missouri was the current location of Hammer's last girlfriend who was in possession of his original reproduction '66 Fender Telecaster guitar. He couldn't play the guitar, but he figured with the money he'd just earned, he could take some lessons. Maybe by someone who'd played in an actual rock band, not some lame high school teacher giving lessons on the side.

He hauled himself up, pulled out his phone, and turned it on. No service, but he could see it was only about ten. He went into the little kitchen and opened the refrigerator. Shit, there were six bricks of marijuana sitting there. He'd forgotten to look in there. No food though. He knew from unloading the other bricks that there wasn't anything else to eat in the RV. In his cooler there were still a couple of beers floating in the melted ice. He opened one and took a long drag. Outside he peed against the tires then sat down on the cabin's rickety steps. What a shit pile. Dwight had said he'd been remodeling the place. It was a dump and those bats in the chimney had almost given him a heart attack. Of course that was a bit of improvisation; he couldn't hide the money in the shed out back like Dwight had said since he'd parked the professor in the outhouse.

He heard something moving around in the little meadow off to the side of the cabin. Jesus, just his luck to get attacked by a bear. He went into the RV and retrieved the Glock. He stood in the doorway peering into the meadow. He could see a dark shape coming toward him and he raised the gun. His heart started racing; if he missed or just wounded it that would only make it mad. He didn't think the RV was strong enough to withstand an angry bear attack. He retreated inside. Maybe it would be a good idea to go into town and find something to eat. If the bear got the professor, then it would be one less thing to worry about.

He climbed into the driver's seat and turned the engine on. The headlights burst out, illuminating the driveway and the figure of a man. Fuck, it was the professor and he was beginning to hoof it down the drive. Hammer opened his door and fired at the professor's retreating back. The shot didn't hit him but it slowed him down and a second bullet plowed into the dirt in front of him and convinced the old man to stop.

"Now, Professor, where the hell did you think you were going? Get your sorry ass back here or the next bullet's going to take off the back of your head."

Nathan lay on the cabin floor breathing dust up his throbbing nose. He didn't think he'd made much progress on the whole escaping thing. He heard the RV start and then idle for a few minutes. Hammer had trussed him up like a hog, the duct tape wrapped tightly around his hands and feet. His legs started cramping, his fingers were raw from trying to get the screws out, and he hoped the cretin hadn't busted his nose. His situation wasn't going to improve when Hammer got back and started to poke around the chimney.

On the highway, Hammer tried to figure out which way was better: Gold Beach or Brookings. He turned on the GPS and decided Brookings was closer. There wasn't much traffic and he rolled into Mickey D's by eleven. The coffee was hot and the big breakfast with sausage, eggs, hash browns, biscuits, and hotcakes went down fine. For dessert he downed a cinnamon melt. He tried to call Sprocket, and then Dwight, but both calls went direct to voicemail. He swung by the Safeway for beer and more provisions. And a double roll of duct tape. It was near midnight when he pulled back onto the highway. He turned the radio up loud and rolled down the window. Cruising on the coast highway would be a lot more fun on his motorcycle instead of this lumbering RV, but he felt good. Almost to the end of the job. By the end of the next day, he'd be cruising down south on his way to freedom and prettier babes.

There was still traffic on the road. The biker rally had really attracted a lot of people. The number of bikers on the road made him uncomfortable. He'd forgotten about the biker who'd bought it. It wasn't like it was his fault a fucking deer walked in front of him. The deer ran off without a scratch on him.

He almost missed the Carpenterville turn off and then he took the turn too fast, barely staying out of the ditch, which kept him from noticing the motorcycle trailing behind him. He started watching the gravel roads off to the right and almost missed the turn onto Bull Gulch Road. He drove a little faster now, a sense of urgency overtaking him. Big clouds of dust from the gravel road billowed out behind him, choking but also obscuring the biker following him. When he turned onto the narrow drive to the cabin he didn't see the biker stop and watch him as he disappeared around the bend. Slowly the biker turned his bike and headed back to the highway, to cell phone coverage, to his buddies.

Back at the cabin, the first thing he noticed was how clean the floor was around the professor. All the dirt seemed to be on the professor, who was looking a little worn out.

"I could use some water."

"I'll say. You smell like shit, Professor. I guess a few hours in the shit house rubbed off on you." He twisted the cap off a PBR and took a draw. He looked back at the professor and decided it would be best to break out that new duct tape. He took Nathan's boots off—wouldn't want him wandering off again. Hammer wrapped a couple more yards of duct tape around Nathan's hands and feet and left him lying on the wood floor. Not before putting a cold beer on the floor next to Nathan.

"Here you go, Professor. Have a beer on me." Hammer laughed. He went outside. He was tired; he was going to sleep like the dead.

Dwight stopped in Brookings just before midnight and bought some food and beer at an all-night gas station. He picked up a local newspaper, not to read but to help start a fire. He doubted Hammer knew how to get a fire going without gasoline and he didn't want his remodeled cabin to go up in flames. It was dark when he pulled onto Bull Gulch Road so he checked the odometer. It was tricky finding the driveway, but it was precisely 1.9 miles to the driveway on the left. Just as he turned, he heard motorcycles screaming up behind him. Their headlights turned into the overgrown driveway across from his. He hoped a biker gang wasn't squatting at the derelict cabin. But, he wasn't going to have to worry about trashy neighbors once he got his hands on the money. He drove slowly on the old gravel driveway and pulled up to a dark cabin. No sign of the RV.

He carried the groceries to the door and found the key under the fake rock by the bottom step. Inside he flicked on the lights and looked around. There wasn't any sign that Hammer had been there. That didn't make any sense. Hammer had left a message yesterday that they had found the cabin and made the transfer. He should be here sitting on a pile of money. Wait! The money should be hidden out back. Dwight started to get a sick feeling in his gut. He grabbed a flashlight and went outside. Behind the cabin was an old garden shed. He opened the door and shone the light on the floor. Under a sheet of plywood was a small hole that should be filled at this moment with almost two million dollars. He picked up the plywood and shined the flashlight down. It was an empty hole. Dwight stood there a full minute before the primal scream ripped through the small clearing. He was going to kill him. He raced to his car and peeled down the driveway. He picked up a signal by the time he made it to Highway 101. Hammer didn't answer his phone and he left a long and creatively profane message on his voicemail. He tried calling Sprocket but it went straight to voicemail too. For all he knew they were in on it together. Fuckers. Morons. Fish bait. On the drive back to the cabin he imagined all sorts of creative ways to slowly murder his cousins.

He had downed four beers when the gunfire started. Probably those biker dudes. A gun, that's what he wanted. He was going to need a gun to deal with the loose end that was named Hammer. Maybe tomorrow he'd go find those bikers and see if they'd sell him a gun. Hammer didn't know what trouble he was in. You don't mess with the Dwight, no siree.

Friday 1:00 a.m.

Nathan thought he was too exhausted to sleep. His shoulders were aching from being tied behind his back and all he could think of was how thirsty he was. The cold beer was an especially cruel touch. He lay for a while dreaming of ways to repay Hammer. But, despite the pleasure of vicarious torture, he found his eyes starting to droop and he let them go. He woke when a light shone in his face. All he could see was a pair of black leather boots.

"Who are you?" A man's voice behind the flashlight.

"I was kidnapped. They stole my RV." His voice was raspy; his throat was so dry.

"Who's 'they'?"

"The guy, Hammer."

"Where are his friends?"

"I don't know. Not here."

"It's just an old man. Leave him, Zach."

"Water. I need water."

The light turned toward the door and Nathan caught a glimpse of a man in motorcycle jacket going down the steps. The flashlight holder took out a pocketknife and cut the duct tape on Nathan's hands and feet.

"Stay put, old man."

Hammer woke when something hard slammed into his face. He felt warm liquid running down his smashed nose. He tried to roll but was too slow and another blow hit his shoulder and he heard a snap. Something in his arm screamed in pain. Another blow missed his head by inches, the crack of something hitting the wall sharp in his ear.

"Enough, Tommy, he's gotta talk to us."

The clubbing stopped and a flashlight shone down. Hands grabbed his feet and pulled him out of the bedroom and out of the RV and onto the ground. A foot rolled him over so the light blinded him and he tried to lift his right arm to shield his eyes but it wasn't working so good.

"Who the hell are you?" He managed a little belligerence in his voice. Big mistake. The club came down hard on his knee.

"Fuck, Tommy. I told you to stop."

"He don't need his knee to talk."

"What if he has to show us where it is? You want to carry him around in the woods?"

A black leather boot toed his legs, "He's okay, aren't you, you piece of shit?"

"What do you guys want?" By now, Hammer's bravado had faded, his voice becoming plaintive.

"What do you think, Einstein? The money. Big dope deal means big money, laying around here somewhere. You want to tell us where you hid it? We'll be out of your hair quick as lightning when you do."

"What money?"

"Don't be stupid, piglet. We know you stole a whole truck-load of top grade marijuana. And we happen to know that you got paid a shitload of money for it."

Hammer looked over to where he could dimly see Nathan sitting with a beer in his hands in the cabin doorway. The fucking professor. Of course he'd rat him out.

"It wasn't my marijuana. It was his. I've been trying to get him to tell me where he hid the money since yesterday. This is his RV."

"What a comedian. That's real funny." One man, Hammer still couldn't see either of their faces, shone the light on Nathan.

"Here we have an old guy, respectable, button-down shirt, a little worse for wear but definitely not scumbag rags. You," the light came back to Hammer, "are a dirty little lowlife pecker with aspirations above your station in life. Fork it over now and save us all a lot of trouble. Tommy here is just aching to have a go at you, after what you did to his brother Ted. You remember the biker you drove into the ditch. Don't make me let Tommy off the leash."

"Please. I didn't hurt anyone. A deer ran out on the road. And the money? I really don't know where it is. My cousin hid it while I was in town. He took off to get another guy. They're going to be back real soon. The other guy, he's trouble man, ain't no way you're going to get anything out of those two. If you was smart you'd clear out now while you had the chance."

"What's your cousin's name?"

Hammer hesitated.

"You just pissed on your last chance."

"Dwight. His name is Dwight. He's a real badass. He's ..."

"He better hurry. Tommy here isn't very patient. Why don't you tell us where the money is now before Tommy slips his chain?"

Hammer looked around, like somewhere in the dark was a posse of friends who could save him. He couldn't bring himself to tell them. It was probably the only big money he'd ever latch onto. You don't let go of a dream that easily. The club, which turned out to be a large branch, came crashing down at the side of his head, sending slivers flying. One of them lodged in his cheek but he hardly noticed it above the pain in his face and shoulder.

"Okay, Tommy. I guess he chooses you. Start with something little, like a few fingers or something."

Hammer whimpered and tried to roll away. A black boot crunched down again on his knee and held him in place. The man called Tommy knelt down and grabbed one of his hands and forced it down on the ground. Then he took the end of the branch and smashed it down hard. Hammer screamed and pulled it back. He rocked back and forth with his hand nestled against his chest.

"Look what I found in the RV." Zach stood in the doorway. He was holding the Glock 39 out in front of him.

"Jesus, don't point that thing. A Glock. Hey, shit for brains, what're doing with that? It's so cute, like a baby glock. Maybe you are some kind of big league criminal." They all laughed at this.

"Let's go see if we can shoot something with the baby gun. Let Tommy do his work in private. Yell when you get something."

Tommy stood over Hammer and started breathing loud. Really loud. He threw in a few chuckles for good effect. He tapped the branch on the ground in a random pattern around the supine Hammer. Hammer was covered in sweat, blood, and grime. He was afraid he was going to pee his pants. Outside, the other men fired off a few rounds and Hammer felt the warm piss fill his pants. The tapping got louder and the breathing got faster. And in the doorway Nathan, started working his way toward the far edge of the porch. When the branch finally made contact with some part of Hammer, Nathan rolled off, Hammer's screams covering any sounds he made.

Outside, Nathan stopped and tried to find where the shooters were playing cowboys. He didn't want to become a dead Indian by accident. He could see the dim outline of the shooters now. They were halfway down the driveway, cutting off that route for escape. He ducked around the corner and crept along the house, nearly tripping over the old bike, but catching himself and the bike before either crashed to the ground. The ground was rough under his stocking feet and he made his way to the rear of the house toward the outhouse. He remembered there was a dirt path that went on past the outhouse toward the forest. It was very dark under the trees. The path he was on was a narrow deer trail that meandered deeper and deeper into the forest. What he wanted to do was to make his way to the road. It was going to be slow going, no shoes, no easy trail, and once he found the road he'd have to stick to the edge of the trees in case the bikers came looking for him. Because he knew, as soon as Hammer broke and told them where the money was hidden, all hell was going to break loose. Because it wasn't hidden there anymore. He almost felt sorry for Hammer.

He jumped when Tommy shouted out to the others that Hammer had spilled the beans. He could just see through the trees the narrow beams of the flashlights jitter bugging inside the cabin. He needed to get off the path. His eyes had adjusted to the dark and he could see a fallen tree further back in the trees. He climbed over that and kept on going to a tree that was leaning almost to the ground, its roots half out of the ground. Behind that, he found a group of evergreen manzanita bushes, which satisfied him. He got down and crawled under the stiff branches. He curled up into himself and sat listening to the shouts coming from the cabin.

"This is shit, man, it's disgusting. I don't see a thing. Get the piglet in here, make him dig around for it."

"His hands aren't working real good right now. This is where he said it was."

"I don't see a fucking thing. Fucking hell." A bat flew out of the chimney and all three men started to wave their arms frantically. The bat flew out the open door.

"Jesus, I think I just swallowed bat shit." Tommy started hawking up blobs of spit and the other two men hopped away from his indiscriminate spitting.

"This is stupid. We can't see nothing."

"Okay, okay. Why don't we take a break? Wait till it gets light. We aren't in a rush here."

The three men went into the RV. Tommy and Mark lit joints and Zach downed a cold beer. They were all tired. Mark took over the bed. Zach sat in the passenger seat and tucked the Glock between the seat and the center console then leaned his head against the window. He was snoring in minutes. Tommy fished another beer out of the cooler and went out to check on the hostages. Inside the cabin he found Hammer curled into a ball, his blood caked hands tucked into his chest. There was no sign of the old man. Tommy stood there a moment wondering if that was a problem. The old man wasn't a player, and certainly wasn't going to get anywhere at night and with no boots. He should probably tell Mark. Thing was, Mark was the kind of guy who shot the messenger. Well, he didn't have to tell anyone he'd found the old man missing. He could act surprised in the morning just like the others.

Chapter Fourteen

The wee hours of Friday morning

Claudie raised her arm to shield her eyes from the bright light, aware of the low rumble coming from the dog. It took her a few seconds to realize that someone was standing by the bed shining a flashlight at her face. Her heart did a backflip and she tried to sit up.

"Shhh. Down, boy." The woman's voice was low and directed to Buddy. The dog's growl faded to just a minor vibration against Claudie's leg. Claudie could smell a strange perfume, musky and spicy, coming from the dark shape.

"So, you're the girlfriend?"

"*Bloody hell.* Who are you? What are you doing here?"

"I'm here to help Nathan of course. Listen, I've had a long day. I'm going to curl up in that comfy looking chair and we can catch up in the morning. Go back to sleep." The light went off and Claudie could just make out someone settling into the chair.

"Jesus. You could have waited till morning, you know."

"The dog seemed concerned about my sudden appearance. I just wanted him to know I'm a friend. Good night."

Claudie, wide awake, lay there until she could hear the woman's breathing become slow and regular. Buddy had long ago fallen asleep. For Claudie it was another hour before the jumble of questions in her brain quieted down enough for her to doze off.

When she woke in the morning it took a minute, and the lingering whiff of the spicy perfume, before she remembered her nighttime guest. She looked over to the chair but it was empty. Maybe it was a dream. The door to the little patio was open and the dog was gone. Morning light spilled in and with it the scent of strong coffee. Claudie hauled herself out of the bed and wrapped a small throw around her. She went to the door and found Buddy sitting by a woman who was reclining in the lounge chair. A cup of gently steaming coffee was perched on the arm of the chair. Her auburn head was looking down on a smartphone screen as her fingers nimbly tapped and scrolled. She looked up and Claudie could see that she was probably in her late thirties, dark eyes speculative as they returned Claudie's gaze.

"Good morning. I'm Dani. There's a pot of tea on the table there. It should still be hot. I used the tea you had in your duffle. Brought cream and sugar if you are so inclined." She looked back down.

Claudie looked back to where her duffle was open by the comfy chair. Then she sat at the table and put her fingers against the teapot. It was still very hot so she poured a cup and did the cream and sugar thing. Buddy came over and she idly stroked his black velvet ears.

"So, Claudie O'Brien," Dani glanced up, "sixty-one, looks more like fifty, she lives in Sisters, that's where I presume you met Nathan. Before that a couple of decades mostly in Portland, with a hopscotch of jobs and other cities sprinkled in, and a number of husbands, all except one, discarded by you. Would I be wrong in in that?"

Claudie shrugged. If Dani wanted to amaze her with her investigative abilities, then have to it.

"Born in Cedar Rapids, Iowa, a four-year stint at the University of Wisconsin, a brief time in Chicago with husband number one, then Portland, then London for a brief time, then Portland without the London husband. Married again and I must say I'm not sure you actually divorced the London guy before you married number two. The divorce records are a little murky on that point. Then you …"

"Dani, I know my history, I don't need a refresher course. Is there a point to this other than to show me how clever you are?"

"My objective is to see how you are involved with my good friend Nathan, and what you know about his disappearance. You want to clue me in on that?"

"I'm just relieved that someone finally believes me when I say something is wrong. How do you know?"

"He texted me. We have little codes worked out whenever we get into a bit of bother. He sent me a text on Thursday morning, the one when translated means 'I need help, come ASAP'. Tell me your story."

Claudie began from the top. When she finished, her tea was cold and Dani was tapping again on the phone screen.

"How is it that you know Nathan?"

"We worked together."

"You were a professor too?"

Dani looked up blankly and then flashed a grin. "Yeah, I taught linguistics."

"In Lebanon?"

"Around there."

"And you have some kind of 'rescue me' code worked out?"

"The Middle East is a tough place. We had a little community of like folk. We watched each other's backs."

"You weren't CIA or something, were you?"

"Really, Claudie, do you know of anyone who would be less likely to be CIA than dear Nathan?"

"Isn't that the point? Aren't CIA types always trying to blend in, not look all sneaky and devious?"

"You insult me, Claudie, just when I thought we were going

to be friends." She stopped tapping, stood, and stretched, only her left arm reaching up, the other she kept gingerly by her side. "Okay, I've got a read on where he was last night. His RV is still there. We need to get going."

"We?"

"Yep. I've got a wee rotator cuff problem. I took a spill on my motorcycle yesterday. I need someone to drive. You'll do, it won't be dangerous, just get me where I need to go and I'll find Nathan. You got anything better to do? I tell you, Mrs. Wesley is having conniption fits about you. A little distance from that woman would be advisable."

"How in the world do you know that?"

"She has one of the most pathetic passwords in the world, and she uses the same one on her phone and computer. She's quite the drama queen."

"You read her emails?"

"Sure, always good to scope out the land. Yours, by the way, is pretty clever, good mix of letters and numbers, and you change it from account to account."

"You read *my* emails?"

"Like I said, I need to know who's who and what's what. Your emails are boring but I like your blog. Get dressed. We can grab something to eat on the way."

"This isn't a car, it's a mobile junk yard. I thought better of you."

"It's loaner from the garage. They shot my car, remember?"

"But, it's so … so yellow. On undercover missions I don't usually like to drive around in such memorable wheels. Let's check out what King has tucked into his garage."

"You mean steal a car from the Wesleys?"

"Borrow. Nathan is family. I would think they'd be happy to lend us a car to rescue him." Dani led Claudie through the silent kitchen and through a door into the garage. She turned on the light and a smile lit up her face. "Will you look at this?" The third car was a bright red Dodge Charger. "Now we're cooking with gas."

"That's hardly inconspicuous."

"Yeah, but it has power. Lots of it. We need to be able to fly, could be some bikers might try to muck up our plan." Dani opened the garage door.

"Swell. Bikers. Only thing is, I can't drive that."

"What do you mean? That's a brand new Dodge Charger Hellcat."

"I think the 'hellcat' says it all."

"You drive a BMW. You can't be a total wuss."

"With my car a little inattention to the accelerator doesn't send me into a sub-orbital flight."

"Oh, yeah, you got to pay attention. But you got me. Pile in. Wait, not the dog."

"I can't just leave him here." Claudie made no move to get Buddy out of the back of the car.

"Why not? He's a dog, not a baby. Tie him up or something. I can't have him barking or running around while I'm trying to take down some bad guys. You wouldn't want him to get shot, would you?"

"Shot? Hell, I don't want to get shot. What are you talking about?"

"Worst case scenario is what. I didn't think you had anything against guns with that little Smith & Wesson in your shoulder bag."

"I wasn't planning on hurting anyone with it. All the bullets are scattershot—it's to make someone reconsider coming in my tent."

"And if they reconsider it with a gun of their own? One with real bullets? It's stupid. You have a gun, you have to be prepared to use it. The first rule they teach you is, if you carry a gun, if you shoot a gun, you better be prepared to kill. A wounded bad guy is an angry bad guy. If not, don't pack it. Who's this?"

"What?" Claudie turned to see who Dani was talking about. Ellie was standing on the driveway looking in at them. She was dressed in purple running shorts and top, bright green running shoes, and yellow socks.

"Good morning, Claudie. Why are you leaving so early? Hey, Buddy." Buddy had bounced out of the car and trotted over to greet her.

"My friend and I are going to look around for Nathan. We were looking for a car with a little more get up and go than my Subaru."

"The Hellcat sure has that. Want me to get the keys?"

"That would be great. You must be Ellie. You may not remember me. I'm a friend of Nathan's. I'm Dani."

"I do remember you! You were with Uncle Nathan and Aunt Kay when I visited him in Rome. You're an artist or something?"

"Artist. Yes, in fact I was driving down the coast doing some sketches for my water colors when Claudie called me."

"I thought you did photography?"

"That too. Listen, Ellie, I'm wondering if you can do us a big favor. Could you watch after Buddy here while we're gone? I hate to drag him around all day in the car."

"Sure thing. Won't that be fun, Buddy?" She bent and received a big sloppy kiss. Claudie felt a twinge of jealousy.

"Okay, that's settled. Let's go Claude." Dani got into the car.

Claudie watched the dog go with Ellie and then got into the luxurious tan leather driver's seat. "Don't call me Claude. My name's Claudette, my friends call me Claudie." Dani shrugged her shoulders, not asking what she should call her. Her perfume lightly spiced the air.

Claudie sat looking at the dashboard. The controls were amazing; dials and gauges everywhere her eye settled. Dani took control of the media center.

"Where to?"

"South on Highway 101. I've got nothing on Nathan's phone but I picked up his RV tracker yesterday in the Brookings area. I'll try to get a read on it now."

"You have a tracker on his RV?"

"Yes. He came down to Austin a couple of years ago and got lost. He has absolutely no sense of direction. I made him put in a GPS system and I customized it with a radio frequency tracking system. Couldn't have my best bud wandering around lost in the desert."

Claudie started the car and the 6.2 liter V–8 Hellcat engine roared to life. She gripped the wheel and inched out of the garage. If she screwed up and they crashed, it would be a hell of a way to go. Putting it in drive she slung gravel all the way down the drive. That'll piss off Mrs. W for sure.

Claudie turned south onto Highway 101 and waited till she was out of town to push the accelerator toward the floor. The ocean flew by on the right.

"That's the ticket, Claudie. I knew you had it in you."

"Yeah, you know so much about me but I know nothing about you. Why don't you tell me more about Dani? Where are you from? I can't place the accent; it's a bit mid-Atlantic. Are you a Brit who's spent a lot of time in the US?"

Dani smiled, "Claudie, I've spent a little bit of time everywhere. I don't really have a home turf, not anymore. It's safer for everyone."

"How very mysterious. How is it that you were nearby when all this happened? Something tells me you weren't really taking pictures of the coast."

Dani laughed. "No. No time for pretty pictures this trip. Let's just say I am hunting for someone who has some information I need."

Claudie glanced at her and thought she wouldn't want to be the person Dani was searching for. There was something steely under the mop of auburn curls and flippant attitude. "When we get where we're going, what are you going to do?"

"Won't know till I get the lay of the land. If we're lucky, Nathan is still in the hands of the amateurs who stole the marijuana."

"And if we're not?"

"Then things will get pretty lively. And if I say 'duck', Claudie, you damn well need to duck."

"Yes ma'am. Roger that."

Chapter Fifteen

Saturday early morning

Nathan woke with a raging thirst and muscles that did not want to respond to his command. He hurt everywhere and he was freezing. He sat and listened to the birds twittering in the trees. The air was chilly and the sky was already light blue, just like it is after the sun crests the horizon. It took him several minutes to decide the direction of the cabin. He couldn't hear anything coming from there. Which told him nothing. He should have stayed awake and tried to slip past the cabin and bikers before it got light. He needed to do a little reconnoitering. He crawled out of the bushes and stood slowly like a flower in slow motion opening up to the sun. He stretched every protesting muscle and got his circulation going again. Still no sounds from the clearing. As silently as he could, he made his way back to the edge of the trees and watched the cabin for a minute. The trouble was, he couldn't see the front door or the RV. He couldn't see any motorcycles either. He had no idea where the men had parked them. That told him a giant nothing too. He wondered how Hammer was doing and if the bikers realized that Hammer was too stupid, and now way too frightened, to lie to them. If so, one of them would surely be bright enough to wonder if the old coot might know something. He looked around the border of the clearing. There had been a wooden fence once, but it was mostly slumped to the ground, rotting slowly along the forest edge. He really wished he'd grabbed his boots. He had already stepped on a few sharp sticks and he had a long way to go. He decided to stay on the forest side of the fence, but close to the sagging posts where it was easier going than inside the trees.

He made it about fifty feet to where he could see the front of the cabin and froze when he spotted one of the bikers lean-ing against the cabin wall by the door. The guy looked like he was sleeping but all he had to do was open his eyes and he'd see Nathan in his peripheral vision. Damn. He couldn't see the other two. They could be in the cabin, but most likely they were in the RV. There were three motorcycles pulled off to the side of the driveway, unfortunately on the other side of the driveway from him. Double damn.

He stepped back behind a tree and began forcing his way through the undergrowth in the general direction of the road. He climbed over a small deadfall and stepped on a very large, and very dry, branch. There was a crack like a small firecracker. He froze, almost afraid to turn and look, not wanting any motion to draw the guy's attention. But of course he looked. The man on the porch was standing now, looking around the clearing but not settling on any one thing. He looked into the cabin and then walked over to the RV and pounded on the passenger window. From his angle, Nathan couldn't see anything, but he used the man's inattention to crouch down. He was now level with the motorcycles and he looked at them speculatively. If the keys had been left with the bikes—better yet, if all three keys were there—then he could toss two away and take off on one of the bikes. Yeah, big ifs. If wishes were horses, etc. etc.

The RV bounced up and down, and he could see one guy get out of the passenger seat. He was holding a beer. Nathan wanted so badly to walk up and grab it; his mouth was so dry he doubted he could spit. The guy drank it down and tossed the bottle into the weeds. A third man finally came into view. He was shorter than the other two, but the way he was barking orders at them, Nathan figured he must be the leader of the pack. They went into the cabin and immediately the leader and the porch guy came back out and stood looking around the clearing. Without a doubt, looking for little old him. They didn't seem anxious at the moment. One of them went into the RV and came back out with a broom. Probably to poke up the chimney. They went back into the cabin.

Nathan rose up and crab walked through the fence and over to the motorcycles. He was one third lucky. Keys dangled from the ignition of one of the motorcycles. The other two were empty. He could hear some shouting now from the cabin. He looked over and saw a few bats fly out of the top of the chimney. In the light of day, it would soon be obvious the plastic bag of money was not where Hammer had claimed it would be. It was now or never. He picked up the motorcycle with the key and started to roll it down the driveway. He hoped to put the RV between him and the cabin. Just as he made it, he heard one clear and urgent shout. "Find the fucker now." Nathan thought it was time for the fucker to start the bike and get the hell out of there. He started the bike and gunned it down the driveway.

He almost wiped out on the first curve. It had been a few years since he'd been on a motorcycle, and he hadn't had a lot of time to familiarize himself with this one. It was a big old Harley Davidson, probably a classic, but heavy and clumsy compared to the Ducati he used to own. But he didn't really have time to continue that line of thought. The driveway was rough and he gunned it too hard. He felt the bike almost lift off and he throttled back, the tires gripped the ground again. He couldn't hear anything over the roar of the engine, and he didn't know if the other two bikes were in pursuit. He could see the end of the driveway and panicked for a second. Right or left? It was a moot question because just as he slowed to make the turn, a bright red Dodge Charger turned into the drive and stopped. He braked too hard and the bike went down. Luckily he had slowed enough that it didn't kill him. He lay staring up at the sky, his head buzzing. His right shoulder, the one he went down on, curiously not feeling anything. Not yet. A head appeared in his vision and he tried to focus on it to make sure it wasn't one of the bikers. He thought maybe he was hallucinating because it looked like Claudie. So sweet of her, he thought.

"Oh my god, Nathan. Are you hurt?" She cupped his face in her hands and looked intently into his eyes. He raised his left hand and brought her face down closer and then he kissed her. Her lips lingered a moment on his, soft and surprised. Someone shouted something behind her and she reared back. He tried to focus but all he could hear now was the sound of motorcycle engines. He could feel the ground rumble with their roar. He thought he heard someone yell, "Get down." He was already down so that seemed redundant but then Claudie suddenly pressed her body down on top of him. This wasn't a vision. How about that? Claudie had come looking for him. And then the next thing he heard was the rapid fire of a gun. Ah, he hoped that was Dani. He shut his eyes for a moment.

Nathan. Nathan, get up. Got to run, dear thing." He opened his eyes and realized that Claudie and Dani were both gripping his arms, trying to pull him to his feet. He sat up and, with a big breath, scrambled to his feet. He felt like he might tumble back, but Claudie kept a firm grip on him and they maneuvered him to the back of the amazing red Dodge. Claudie got in the driver's seat and Dani ran around to the passenger side and the car suddenly thundered backward and then whipped around and flew down the road. He caught a brief glimpse of three motorcycles laying down in the drive. He didn't see any bodies. That was too bad.

"Does Brookings have a hospital?" Dani was screaming to them.

Nathan started to shrug and that's when his shoulder began to send urgent pain messages to his brain. He groaned loudly and Claudie looked at him over her shoulders and then turned to the front.

"If they have one it won't be large. Do you think those guys are going to follow us? Nathan needs help right away."

"All I did was annoy those guys. And they looked pretty mad already. *Nathan.*"

Nathan looked up at her. She was twisted around watching the road behind them. He felt so dopey. Maybe he hit his head on something. Oh, yeah, the road.

"Those guys? Why are they chasing you? Are they going to keep coming?"

Nathan thought for a moment, a smile slowly spread across his face.

"Most definitely." He swayed, leaning forward as Claudie

finally reached the highway and turned south toward Brookings. "I've got the money."

"Money? What money? Where?"

Dani patted his shirt as if he could have the money on him. It made him laugh. "Not on me. You know me, Dani, I'm good at finding money. Although usually not in the actual literal physical sense of finding it. One million eight hundred thousand dollars, or thereabouts. Do you have any idea how heavy that much money is? I myself had no idea." Claudie had to brake hard for a lumbering RV and the smile left his face.

"Nathan, what about the money? What are you talking about?" Dani was watching him in the rear view mirror. Her eyes roamed from the highway in front to the highway behind them and paused a second on his face. He smiled at her. Good old Dani. His head swung around to Claudie. He'd kiss her again but everyone seemed to be in such a bother. Oh, the money.

"I hid it. Hammer hid it in the chimney and I got it out and I hid it. He never knew. They all think I'm just a silly old professor. I fooled them." He swung his head back to Claudie and thought about kissing her again, but it was too much effort to lean forward. She seemed to be real busy driving.

"Where'd you hide the money? Nathan? Shit."

The car surged forward around a pick-up pulling a long trailer.

"Are they following us?" Claudie looked back through the rear window.

"I can't tell. Those guys have buddies everywhere. We need to get Nathan to the hospital first."

Nathan looked puzzled. "I can't remember."

"You can't remember what, Nathan?"

"Where I hid the money. Isn't that strange?"

"It certainly makes things more challenging."

They hit the city limits and Claudie hardly slowed. At a stop light by the Fred Meyer, Dani pointed out the blue sign for the hospital. Claudie screeched to a halt in an "emergency vehicles only" spot in front and Dani raced in. Claudie waited in the car. Nathan sat quietly, his chin grazing his chest.

Claudie heard a motorcycle cruise by and she twisted around to watch a red Harley with a black leather-clad biker drive by. Almost politely. Too politely. There was a police station a couple of blocks away. Both the hospital and the police station were off the main highway. No reason for a stray biker to take this street. He didn't seem to pay any attention to the car, but the bright red Dodge Charger wasn't hard to miss. Finally Dani came out followed by an attendant with a wheelchair.

Claudie stayed at the hospital with Nathan and waited for a doctor to see him. Dani disappeared, something to do with the car. Nathan wasn't completely coherent and the waiting room was very busy. The biker rally was throwing the entire medical and law enforcement community in Southern Oregon for a loop. She heard a nurse gripe about how ineffectual the county was. No permit had been granted for the event, but that hadn't stopped nearly two hundred bikers from descending onto the beach.

The doctor who finally treated Nathan was more concerned about a possible concussion than his shoulder. Dani showed up as the doctor finished his lecture. They were to keep an eye on Nathan at all times. He could sleep, but they should wake him every couple of hours to make sure he was doing okay. Dani led them to a side entrance and made them wait while she scanned the parking lot.

Once back, she said, "I booked you a room at the Brookings Motor Lodge. You can get him cleaned up and keep tabs on him." She handed Claudie a bag of new clothes.

"Aren't we going back to Gold Beach?"

"And drag a biker gang there in time for the wedding?" Dani looked out the door again, a little too anxiously for Claudie's comfort. Nathan was sitting in a wheelchair with a dazed look in his eyes.

"Why would they still be after us?"

"I can think of one million eight hundred thousand reasons."

"But they must know we'll go to the police ..."

"What? Nathan's too out of it to talk to the police. And he doesn't seem to remember where he hid the money. As far as the biker boys think, Nathan's a crook and the money is still up for grabs. Nathan is the pied piper who will lead them to it. Here's your taxi."

"Aren't you coming with us?"

"No. Right now that red Dodge Charger is the focus of their attention. I've got to tuck it away someplace inconspicuous. Pick up another set of wheels. When Nathan here is coherent enough, you can tell the cops all about it. Then our biker friends will lose interest and go back to smoking dope and lighting bonfires on the beach."

"Nathan? You about finished in there?" Claudie stood outside the bathroom door listening to the water still running in the shower. It shut off and Claudie listened for a minute more and then realized she didn't want him to come out and find her standing right there. He hadn't taken the bag of clothes in with him so she put it right by the door and went out to the little balcony. They were on the second floor and had a good view of the ocean. The morning fog had lifted and the sky and ocean were brilliantly blue. She heard rustling behind her and turned to see a naked Nathan pulling back the bedcovers and climbing in.

"How are you feeling?" Claudie sat on the second queen-sized bed.

Nathan opened his eyes and looked surprised to see her.

"I keep thinking you're a dream. You came looking for me." He had a note of wonder in his voice.

"Of course. You owe me a cup of coffee."

"Tea. You like tea. And wine."

"It's a little early for wine, even for me. You need to rest. I'll be right here."

"Where's Dani?"

"She's out trying to throw the scent off. Those bikers could still try to grab you. You still don't remember where you hid the money?"

Nathan shook his head. His eyes were at half-mast so Claudie stopped asking questions and let him fall asleep. She sat watching him for a while and her hand came up and brushed her lips. The memory of his kiss was soft and sweet. The surprise wasn't just about what he'd done. It was also how she felt. She hadn't expected to feel like that ever again in her life; that warm sexual tingle that started way down deep in her body. She sighed and then went back out to the balcony. The ocean was calm and the tide was receding. She looked out to the ocean and breathed the first easy breath she'd taken since Thursday morning. It felt good that it was over.

Chapter Sixteen

Friday morning

Dwight jerked awake. Bright sunlight spilled into the cabin and stabbed needles into his eyes. He'd rounded out the previous night with half a bottle of bourbon. He heard a loud bang. Shit, that sounded like a gun. He remembered the guys shooting last night. What jerk faces. He took a deep breath and sat up. And that made his head throb like the devil. He thought about going back to sleep, but a sense of urgency about the money chased the lethargy away. He needed to find that asshole Hammer and get his money. If the moron was trying to stiff him, he was going to be in for a surprise. He listened but didn't hear any more gunshots. He'd mosey on down and see if he could buy himself some firepower.

Fortified with a Red Bull, Dwight got in his Malibu and headed out in search of the idiots with guns. The driveway opposite his had a lot of recently spewed up dirt and gravel. It had to be where the bikers had turned down last night. He turned in and drove cautiously for about a half a mile before coming into a small meadow with a rundown cabin. There was a small RV parked in front but no motorcycles in sight. He parked and walked around the RV. The side door was wide open and after calling out hello, he poked his head in. It was a shambles inside. The cabinet doors were hanging open and there was the unmistakable smell of marijuana hanging in the air. Jesus, this must be the RV that Hammer was driving. He stepped in and did a quick once over. There was no sign of the money. But he did find a gun. Slipped in beside the passenger seat was a little Glock. Nice.

He got out and looked the cabin over. The door to it was open also.

"*Hammer*! Hammer, are you in there?" It was dark and still inside the cabin and he slowly stepped up to the porch and looked in. It took a moment for his eyes to adjust, and another moment to realize that the jumble on the floor by the fireplace was a human being. He approached warily. Looking down, he could just recognize Hammer. His face was swollen and so bloody and discolored that it wasn't what Dwight recognized. It was the round pumpkin head that sat glumly on his shoulders. He hesitated and then forced himself to kneel down and touch Hammer's nearly non-existent neck. It was warm and he could feel a pulse. The asshole was alive. Relief washed over Dwight's tense frame. It wasn't concern over Hammer's welfare. He needed this pile of shit to tell him where the money was. Dwight had a bad feeling that it could be in the possession of a gang of bikers, or whoever the idiots were who had beat the pulp out of Hammer. Hammer twitched away from Dwight's hand and he made a sound that was almost like sobbing.

"Ham, it's me. Dwight. I'm here to help you, buddy."

Hammer tried to open his eyes but Dwight could see only a sliver of one eyeball looking up at him.

"Let me get you something to drink." He went out to the RV and checked the ice chest on the floor behind the driver's seat. One lone beer floated in the cool water. He opened it and took a long swig. He took it back to Hammer and held it to his lips. Most of it dribbled down his shirt before Hammer opened his mouth enough to drink. It set off a coughing fit that caused Hammer to clutch at his torso. Dwight figured the bikers had done a thorough job of pummeling Hammer. The man was bruised and bloodied, and he was having trouble breathing, probably a few ribs broken, maybe a punctured lung. And by the look of his hands, a good number of fingers were smashed.

"Bikers ..." Hammer croaked the words, barely above a whisper.

"They're gone. Did they get the money?"

Hammer's one eye closed and he seemed to drift off. Dwight shook him.

"Hammer. Where's the money? Tell me where it is and we can go." Hammer's lips moved. There were small pink bubbles in the corners of his mouth.

"The professor. He took it." It was barely a whisper.

"What professor?"

"The bastard … hid it …" Hammer took a painful breath. "Should … have … let the bears eat him." He coughed and more pink bubbles dribbled out of his mouth. Hammer was useless to him.

Dwight walked back to the RV and went inside. He opened the glove box and pulled out the registration. Nathan Forest and he lived in Sisters. He tucked it back into the glove box and then he did one more inspection of the RV. The closet and cupboards were empty, there was a brick of marijuana that had been split open, the grass scattered all over the table. Just before leaving he opened the refrigerator to look for something else to drink. Sitting on the bottom shelf were five intact bricks of marijuana. He scooped them up and went back to his car. Past time to go. He gunned it down the long driveway, and laughed to himself when he thought about what would have happened if he'd shown up and asked the bikers for a gun. A lucky break for him. At the road he stopped. A twinge of conscience, should he take Hammer to the hospital in Brookings? But there'd be a lot of questions that would inevitably lead to jail. There was a chance that he could find out what happened to the money if he acted fast. He looked in the rear view mirror. It wasn't a hard choice for him. After all his hard work and planning, he chose the money.

Friday morning

Sprocket woke to the sound of motorcycles revving their engines. He was slumped against the passenger door of his truck, his neck aching from the odd angle he'd been in since Aileen left him there last night. She'd taken the keys and went in search of her stupid guitar player. He sat up straighter and looked around. The windshield was all fogged so he unrolled the window and could just barely hear the ocean over the sound of motorcycle engines. The truck was parked on the side of the highway where the highway hugged the beach. Just north there was a horse trail that curved into forest. It ran toward the ocean and away from the coast highway. Motorcycles were lazily rolling down this trail. Sprocket could distantly remember camping on a beach around here one summer. He thought it could be where the bikers were headed. He yawned and looked in the back to see if Aileen had left any food. There was a sack with a few French fries in it and he ate those. He groped under the seat and found a five-hour energy drink and downed it. A little caffeine would help. He didn't know what else to do. He didn't want to leave the truck. Hammer's motorcycle might be too tempting to this crowd. And if anyone started digging under that tarp they might find a treasure way more valuable. That treasure represented his new life and he wasn't going to leave it behind now.

He got out and stretched. There was still a layer of morning fog hugging the beach but it was thin and he figured it would burn off. It'd get hot then. He started to climb down to the sand when he heard his name being called.

"Sprocket. Wait."

He looked back along the trail and saw Aileen trudging toward him with a large backpack on her shoulders. At the truck she threw it into the back and climbed into the driver's seat.

"Let's go. I need to pick up some food and beer. I thought we could go into Gold Beach and look around."

Sprocket grumbled a little about not being allowed to drive his own truck but Aileen gave him one ball-breaking look and he shut up. He was going to be nice if it killed him. For once in his life he was going to keep the end goal in sight and not fuck it up before reaching it. He was going to keep his temper if it killed him.

They drove aimlessly around Gold Beach for a while. Sprocket tried to call Hammer but it went straight to voicemail. Aileen stopped at a grocery store and he followed her in, pushing the cart behind her as she piled in deli snacks and a couple six-packs of foreign beer. The turd guitar player was too good for Budd or Miller. At the checkout, Aileen chatted with the clerk and then when the groceries were totaled

Aileen looked at him expectantly. The clerk waited with the beginning of a sneer lifting his upper lip so Sprocket pulled out his wallet and paid. Asswipe clerk.

"Okay, Sprocket. I'm heading back. Let's roll that motorcycle out of the back and you can use that to search."

"Hammer doesn't let anyone drive his bike, Aileen."

"Hammer isn't here, Sprocket. And you aren't going to find Jasper on foot. Let's go."

"What are you going to do with the truck? You can't leave this stuff parked on the side of the highway."

"Don't worry your cotton candy head about it, Sprocket. I got a plan. You just find my dog."

Sprocket struggled to keep from boiling over and concentrated on getting the motorcycle out of the truck without letting the tarp blow off the dope. But a gust of ocean breeze billowed the plastic up, revealing a couple of empty produce boxes. It wasn't his future lined up all nice and neat under the tarp. It was another Aileen lie. Aileen started the truck and shouted "Oops!" out the window. For fifteen minutes, he screamed to the blue sky about the treachery of cheating women. Finally Sprocket calmed down enough to try to get the motorcycle to start. Fuck, shit, piss on the whole crap world. It wouldn't start. Hammer was never one to waste time on maintenance and the bike did not want to fire up. Sprocket rolled it to a far corner of the parking lot and began to inspect it. It took him about an hour to figure out what the problem was and then he had to go search for parts. He was starving too. He stopped for a burger and fries and then found a place that sold him the parts he needed. It was while he was walking back that he took the time to look around the town. Where he was, the businesses hugged a narrow strip along the highway. The streets on the east side rose steeply with increasingly larger homes commanding the best views. His eye was drawn to a three-story mansion at the top. Boy, wouldn't something like that be grand. He stopped. His mouth was slightly open as he took in the details. The view those people must have. And there, off to the side of the house, by a little red horse trailer, was a bright neon yellow car. He stared at that car and couldn't believe that his luck might have changed. It was the old lady's car. It had to be. He laughed. Payback was coming for that bitch.

Chapter Seventeen

Friday late morning

Claudie didn't hear Dani come in until she was standing in the balcony door. She nearly came out of her skin when Dani asked if she wanted something to eat.

"*Gah!*"

"Is that a yes or no?"

"You scared the bejesus out of me." Claudie went inside where Dani had dumped some fast food containers on the little table. She was so famished that the hot greasy smell started her stomach growling. Dani leaned over Nathan and gently shook his shoulder.

"Owwwww." Nathan swatted at her hand.

"Sorry. You awake enough to eat?"

Nathan said something that was unintelligible and closed his eyes. Dani went over to the table and picked up a sack and a cold drink and went out to the balcony. Claudie took a drink over to Nathan.

"Nathan, here's something to drink. Do you want a pain pill?"

"No." He did open his eyes, and then struggled to pull himself into a sitting position. He accepted the cold drink and took a sip.

"God, it's diet." He set it on the bedstand and looked at Claudie perched on the edge of the other bed. "Why do women always drink diet drinks?"

"I don't know. Maybe because men don't like fat women. You could write a philosophical paper on the conundrum, why men don't like women who drink diet soft drinks but also don't like fat women."

"I'll just leave it as a catch-22."

"How do you feel?"

"Hunky dory. Like someone who spent a day duct taped to a chair, part of the night trapped in an outhouse, and the rest of the night sleeping under a bush."

Claudie laughed and then quickly covered her mouth. "I'm sorry. I always think I have bad experiences camping but you really take the prize."

"Speaking of prizes, you remember where the money

is yet?" Dani stood in the balcony doorway eating from a French fry container.

"I'm beginning to believe I imagined the whole thing."

"Oh, no. The bikers hi-jacked the guy who bought the marijuana. Money definitely changed hands."

"How do you know this?"

"I've spent the last week or so making new friends."

"Did you see any of them when you were out?" Claudie asked, a sense of unease intruding on her relief at finding Nathan.

"There's bikers all over the damn place. That biker shindig going on up the coast. It has the local constabulary in a total tizzy. We aren't going to get any help from those guys. You two need to finish eating and then we're packing up."

"I thought you said it would be better to stay down here?"

"We've lost their scent for now. I don't want to give them time to suss us out. I found us another car. I think we can fly under their radar and get the hell out of here. Nathan?"

"I'm for getting the hell out of Dodge." He threw back the covers to get out of bed and realized he was naked. "Oops." He pulled the sheet back over him.

"*Whooo.* Way too much information, old man. Claudie, where's his duds?"

"Please don't call me old man. I've spent two days with low, two-digit IQ scumbags calling me old and feeble and I've had my fill." He accepted the bag from Claudie and the two women went out to the balcony so he could dress.

Claudie ignored the smirk on the clerk's face when she turned in the key after just a couple of hours. Outside the motel office she got into the passenger seat of a silver Honda. It was quite a comedown from the Dodge Charger. But as Dani pointed out, no one noticed old silver Hondas. They were the most invisible cars on the road. She hoped that was true when they passed the bikers in the Pistol River area. Any one of these tattooed beefy guys could have been the ones at the cabin. Nathan kept his head down and they drove into Gold Beach with relief writ large on their faces.

Friday afternoon

Dwight needed to find out what happened to the money. Hammer hadn't made any sense with "the professor, the fucking professor", and shit like that. Dwight doubted that any of the bikers went by the name of "professor". He had the RV registration. This Nathan could be the professor. But Sprocket had said the guy was an old man. How could some old geezer, some college puff, steal the money out from under Hammer and those bikers? He toyed with the idea of going back to the other cabin but he was afraid the bikers might return. The five bricks of marijuana in the trunk of his car was a pretty piss poor return on all the work he'd put into this job. There was always the dope in the back of Sprocket's truck. It was looking pretty good now. He needed to call Sprocket and find out what was happening on that end. Maybe the moron had found the dog and he had the dope back. He hoped that

Sprocket wasn't dumb enough to hand over the dog without having control of the grass. Aileen sounded like one prize bitch. Way over Sprocket's pay grade.

After days of missed calls, Dwight was surprised that Sprocket answered on the third ring.

"Where are you?"

"Gold Beach. You aren't going to believe me. I'm looking at the old lady's car. It's parked up at a house on the cliff over the town. I'm going up there now to get that stupid dog and if the old lady tries to stop me, then she's going to get what she has coming to her." Sprocket was so excited his voice went up an octave.

"Wait, wait. Don't go off half-cocked. Do you have a plan? Or are you just going to knock on the door and ask for the dog? Something tells me that won't work."

"*It's my fucking dog, Dwight.* Jesus. That old bat stole my dog. She hasn't any right to it. I could call the cops on her …"

"*Sprocket.* What are you thinking? Calling the cops?" Dwight laughed. "Like they would take your word over hers."

"Okay. I'll sneak up later when it gets dark."

"That sounds better. Have you been in touch with Aileen? Do you know where the truck is at?"

"Kind of. We drove down here together. She was meeting that guitar player at the biker rally …"

"You drove down there with her? In the truck?"

"Yeah." Sprocket drew the word out.

"You were riding in your own damn truck and you didn't

just take the keys away from her and dump her sorry ass?"

"I would never hurt Aileen, Dwight. I still care for her. That guitar player is going to …"

"That guitar player is probably smoking our dope and selling it to all his buddies. Jesus fucking Christ."

Sprocket heard Dwight take three deep breaths.

"Okay. I'm coming up. I'm only about an hour away. You stay put, don't do anything without me."

It took Dwight longer than an hour. Back on Highway 101, he headed north along with a troop of motorcycles and lumbering RVs. He passed a bunch of cop cars parked along the highway in the Pistol River area. If the cops had ever imagined that they could control the bikers, it was now clear to them that it was way beyond their manpower. Leather-vested motorcyclists drove slowly past the cops standing at the trailhead. Girls on the back of the bikes were flashing their boobs and screaming with laughter at the hapless cops. It almost looked like fun. And then he thought that the bikers who'd half killed Hammer were probably down that trail already. Maybe with his money.

He followed a silver Honda into town until he found Sprocket hanging outside one of the taverns on the main drag.

"Get in."

"Where's Hammer?"

"Back at the cabin. He's not feeling too good."

"What happened?"

"Bikers, that's what. Like your girlfriend's buddies. They beat him up and took the money."

"Is he hurt bad?"

"He'll be fine. He was never pretty to begin with."

"Damn. The money's gone? Shit." Sprocket heaved himself back into his seat. "What are you going to do?"

"First thing is find a room or something. Hammer wasn't able to tell me exactly what happened yet. He kept saying something about some professor when I found him. You know anything about that?"

"Nah. Unless it was that old guy we took the RV from."

"I didn't see any old guy at the cabin. I wonder if the bikers took him?" Dwight pulled out onto the highway again and headed to a Motel 6 that he'd noticed coming into town.

There was one room left at the Motel 6, and the parking lot was full of motorcycles, which made Dwight very nervous. But it couldn't be helped. You couldn't spit without hitting a biker, and a sane person didn't even look cross-eyed at a biker, let alone lob bodily fluid at them. Unless you had a death wish. Sprocket pointed out the yellow car in the fading light. It was without a doubt Hoyt's loaner Subaru. Now all they had to do was find out where the dog was kept and go nab it. A fancy house like that, the people probably kept their dogs outside in deluxe kennels. They'd wait till it got dark and things quieted down.

Once again, Claudie arrived at the King household in time

for an argument. Mother and daughter disengaged when Nathan came into the kitchen. Ellie squealed and enveloped Nathan in a giant hug. Nathan grimaced but endured it. Claudie noticed the stack of bright yellow colanders on the table. They were filled with spaghetti balls dyed a bright turquoise hue. There were a couple of spools of floral patterned ribbon beside them and a young woman was playing around with ways to tie bows on the colanders.

"Claudie, you found him. You are awesome. Come look at the centerpieces. What do you think?" Ellie still had Nathan by the arm and they all looked down on the most imaginative decorations that Claudie had ever seen.

"Stunning. I never thought you could do so much with plain spaghetti." Nathan clearly loved his niece, Claudie thought.

Mrs. W snorted in the background. They ignored her.

"You were absolutely right about using regular spaghetti, Claudie. What do you think, Uncle Nathan? I'm putting them on the tables tonight for the rehearsal dinner. I am so, so glad you made it in time."

"Nate! I'll be damned. You look like you've been chewed up and spit out by one of those biker thugs. What did you do to yourself?" King stood in front of Nathan, eyeing his cheap, ill-fitting clothes, and the purple bruise on his forehead. King was nattily outfitted in Brooks Brothers casual, every crease crisply ironed.

"King, leave the poor man alone. Ellie, let the man sit down for heaven's sake. Now, tell us what happened. Your friend here," Mrs. W briefly glanced at Claudie, "has told us the most amazing story. And who is that?" She was looking out the kitchen door where Dani was busy on her cell phone. "Don't tell me you have another girlfriend? Isn't that a little …"

"Mother, don't be rude. Claudie's his new girlfriend. Dani was the woman in Rome I told you about. The artist I met when I visited him in Italy."

Nathan looked at Claudie, questions in his eyes, and she felt a hot flush suffuse her face. He took a glass of wine from King and then spent the next few minutes summarizing his adventure. While they peppered him with questions, Claudie looked about for Buddy. She had expected him to be underfoot. She went outside and looked around. Dani was still engrossed in her phone. Claudie took the path to the trailer and heard whining before she saw the dog. Buddy was tied up in the patio area. He'd managed to circle around the awning pole and lounge chair so much that he was tangled with no slack in the leash. But, it didn't stop him from trying to leap toward her. The awning was about to crash by the time Claudie knelt by him and accepted his joyful kisses. She unhooked him from the leash and sat on the chair while he gradually calmed down.

"That dog is sure attached to you. Didn't you say you just got him?" Dani had snuck up on her again. She was holding a bottle of red wine and a couple of glasses.

"I don't think he was happy with the guy who had him. Why aren't you back there soaking up glory?"

"Not my cup of tea, that whole family reunion type thing. Besides, Nathan's sanitized it so much, you'd think that he'd just hitchhiked with a couple of nitwits, not been kidnapped by drug thieves."

"I suspect that he's kept a lot from his family over the years. Now that we're all safe and sound, how about telling me about the work you used to do with Nathan in the Middle East?"

"Middle East? Did I mention the Middle East? Scary place, too rich for my blood. Just like Ellie said, I'm an artist and I knew Nathan in Rome. His wife Kay liked my work and we got to know each other. When Kay got sick, Nathan wanted to come back home and settle into a quiet life. I never thought he'd stay after she died, but he did. He must have found some other interests to keep him in Oregon."

Dani grinned at her. Claudie was tired of protesting the girlfriend trope and was glad she was silent because Nathan appeared bearing another bottle of red wine, a baguette, and an appetizer tray he'd purloined from the kitchen island.

"Ah, ha. Found you girls. Yes, dog, so you like me now, huh?" Nathan managed to sit down at the little table without Buddy tripping him.

"Why aren't you in the bosom of your loving family?" Dani arched a mocking eyebrow at him.

"Ellie's future in-laws have arrived, along with a pack of

young people and it's complete chaos up there. I'm not going back till they put out the food." He poured a tall glass of wine and began tearing off hunks of the crusty bread. They all dived into the tray of cheeses and marinated vegetables and sat drinking and chewing, watching the sun slip down into the sea.

Chapter Eighteen
Friday Night

Dwight and Sprocket drove up the hill looking for the big house. They were flummoxed when they turned the last bend and found the house all lit up like a Christmas tree and half-a-dozen cars parked in the drive. Dwight cursed. They were having a damn party. He reversed the Malibu and parked it about a block down the hill.

"Come on. Let's go take a look. If we're lucky they'll be so busy drinking their Chardonnay they won't notice us."

They paused at the end of the driveway and Dwight looked to the right where he figured the trailer and yellow car were parked. He could see a narrow gravel track along a hedge and they walked down, hugging the far side of the evergreens to stay out of the house lights. They could hear talking and laughing as they approached the end, near the cliff edge. They listened for a while and Dwight was rewarded with the best news of the day. Not only were they going to get the dog back, they had a shot at getting the money back too. Sprocket almost charged in but Dwight restrained him. Patience. Dwight thought picking them off one at a time would be safer. There was an unknown woman with them and he wasn't sure they could handle three people plus the dog.

"I'm fine, Nathan. Really. I'd feel out of place at this family shindig. And look at me, I'm dressed for camping, not a fancy rehearsal dinner." Claudie stood and indicated her worn jeans, tee-shirt, and flannel shirt.

"You look fine to me."

"Ask your sister-in-law what she thinks. I don't think she'd even let me clean her house, let alone sit down at her fancy dinner."

"I don't give a rip about what she thinks. Ellie and King want you to come up."

"That's gracious of them. But, no. Please, I've had plenty to eat and drink and all I want to do is take Buddy for a walk on the beach and then crash. I'm exhausted."

Nathan looked at Dani, "What about you, Dani?"

"Lord no, Professor. I'd probably end up telling them what

I think about the institution of marriage. You'd end up with two persona-non-grata guests to explain. I'm with Claudie. Not the walking the dog on the beach thing, but I could use about a million hours of sleep. Wake me after the young folk get married and before they get a divorce. That's not a long time in America." Dani picked up her phone and started texting again.

"I hate to leave you." Nathan did look unhappy. To Claudie's surprise he gave her a long hug and then disappeared up to the house.

"Wow. Like a house on fire, you two."

"Shut up." She ignored Dani's snort.

"How long are you going to be?"

"Not long. Maybe an hour at max."

"Take your gun. Lots of bad boys out there."

Claudie thought about another glass of wine but decided to wait till after her walk. "Come on, Buddy, let's hit the beach." She ignored Dani's advice about the gun.

The night was clear and chilly. She couldn't see many stars yet. There was too much ambient light from the businesses in town. She could hear the rumble of motorcycles on the highway and wondered if there was a way to avoid the main drag. The hill down was steep and the thought of walking back up tempered her wish to walk in the sand. Perhaps she'd save the beach walk till the next day. A short way down she came to a small park, the Collier H. Buffington Memorial Park. She wondered what Collier H. Buffington had done to deserve a park to himself. It looked green and quiet and she decided to take a stroll around it and then go back up. She passed an empty parking lot and then a picnic pavilion and some tennis courts. Further on was a large play area. Buddy stayed right at her side except once when he did his business close to the edge of the trees. She did her duty and picked it up. She realized she was done in, completely knackered, and she turned around. In the playground she passed a red Malibu. Buddy started growling, deep and loud. She turned to find a skinny man standing behind her. Her arm was jerked back and she turned again to find Buddy pulling on the leash, trying to get to a very large man standing ten feet back. She definitely recognized him, the no neck, round head, and angry glare. It was the guy from the campground, the one who tried to break into her car and take Buddy. Now she was afraid. She kept a strong hold on the leash. Neither of the men seemed eager to approach her with the hostile dog straining on the leash. Buddy had developed some courage in the last few days. But she didn't have time to feel proud of him.

"You're coming with us, lady. And if you don't want the dog hurt you better keep him calm." The skinny man pointed at the red Malibu.

"You're crazy if you think I'm going anywhere with you. You two need to get out of my way."

"Or what, you old bitch? I should shoot you now and be done with it." Sprocket had a gun out now and was vaguely pointing it at Claudie and Buddy. Dwight moved to the side to keep out of the line of fire.

"Come on, be smart. We aren't going to hurt you. We just need a little chat with your friend, the Professor. He has something we want."

It didn't take Claudie long to make the connection. They were after the money. The money Nathan had hid, the money hidden someplace he couldn't remember. Now she was very afraid. These men had worked hard to get what they wanted. She doubted that they were going to give up on their goal now. She, Buddy, and Nathan were obstacles, disposable obstacles.

At the car they made her coax Buddy into the trunk of the car. It broke her heart as the lid slammed down and he started whining. They forced her into the back of the car and they drove to a Motel 6. They handed her a phone and told her to call Nathan. It went to voicemail. She told them she was going to leave a text and Dwight watched her type it in and read it before she hit send. He didn't notice that it went to Dani, not Nathan. It was time for the boys to meet Dani.

"Damn, I should put homing devices on you two." Dani led Nathan back to the horse trailer. Neither one of them was walking a perfectly straight line.

"If I'd known I was going to have to rescue one of you again I wouldn't have drunk all that wine." She poured them both coffee from the carafe she'd taken from the kitchen. "Drink up, we've got a long night ahead of us."

"She can't be that far away, she's only been gone for an hour. When did you get the text?" Nathan sipped the hot coffee gingerly. Waking up wasn't what he wanted to do.

"Five minutes before I dragged you away from that mid-western jamboree you had going there. No wonder the kids all bailed. Even one of this town's tourist pubs would have more life. Now Nathan, I need you to concentrate on that money. They aren't going to hand off Claudie until they verify that you've told them the truth. Can you walk it through in your mind? You remember pulling the money out of the chimney?"

"God, yes. It's not every day that one has bat guano rain down on their face." Nathan frowned and looked out toward the black ocean. "I remember dragging the plastic bag through some grass to get some of the crap off. It was dark. I thought I saw some headlights through the trees so I headed out back. The lights went on but I needed to hurry. I wanted to hike down to the road before Hammer woke up. There's isolated cabins along the road, I hoped to find one and lay low till morning."

"Why didn't you take the money with you?"

"It was too heavy, it would slow me down. Plus, if I got caught, I wanted something with which to bargain."

"Okay, you're walking out back. Into the trees?"

"No, the bag was too bulky to slog down the deer trail. I went into the meadow." He paused.

"And? Come on, you do realize that these guys are threatening to kill her?"

"Dani, shut up, I'm thinking. And I know the stakes."

"Give me your phone, I'll text back to them and find out how they want to play this."

Nathan stood up suddenly, "There's an old metal water trough, for cattle or horses. I tipped it over and put the money under that."

"Not exactly a difficult spot for them to find."

"We're not dealing with rocket scientists. All I had to do was be gone and they'd think I'd taken it. I figured they wouldn't look around too hard. Now what?"

"We wait."

Claudie sat on a supremely uncomfortable chair in a dim corner away from the door. Sprocket sat at the small table by the window and tried to get his girlfriend on the phone. She was piecing some of it together. Buddy belonged to the girlfriend and the girlfriend had something that Dwight and Sprocket wanted badly. This hostage situation had layer upon layer. She wondered what would happen if Nathan couldn't remember. She knew that head injuries could leave people fuzzy for days, if not weeks. Zero patience. That's the point these creeps were at.

Dwight was fidgety. He checked her phone every few minutes. It was nearly midnight and the men had been drinking beer, a lot of it by the smell of them. She thought about Dani and Nathan. They were probably well lubricated too. Great, a bunch of drunks trying to pull off a dangerous exchange, with guns. Christ, someone was going to get killed.

Suddenly there was a loud pounding on the motel door. Everyone levitated about six inches out of their chairs. Sprocket nudged the window curtain aside and looked at Dwight.

"Some dude."

There was another slam on the door and they could hear the guy yelling. The only word Claudie understood was dog. Dwight nodded to Sprocket who picked up the gun and put it in his lap. Dwight opened the door and Claudie could hear it now. A mournful howl was coming from the trunk of the Malibu.

"What the fuck. You guys locked a dog in the trunk of your car? What kind of dickwads do that to a dog?" The man was tall and angry and in Dwight's face.

"The dog bit my cousin. It was the only safe place to put him."

"I don't care if the dog chewed his dick off. You let that dog out or I'm kicking the shit out of your car."

Dwight looked down at the thick black leather boots, shit kickers if he'd ever seen them, and pulled out his keys. He tossed them to Sprocket and Sprocket tossed them right back.

"You get him, Dwight. He hates me."

He brushed past the man and went to the back of his car where the howling continued unremittingly. Sprocket stood in the doorway, one hand braced against the doorframe, the other hand behind his back. Claudie rushed to the door and tried to scoot under his arm but Sprocket's big mitt came down on her head and stopped her. The black booted man stood to the side; he kept an eye on Sprocket while Dwight opened the trunk. Buddy leaped out and immediately sighted Claudie and dashed to her. He nearly knocked her over trying to jump in her face and kiss her. She pulled him back into the room and to her safe corner.

The biker looked hard at Sprocket. "Yeah, that's one vicious dog. Looks like the old lady's going to keep it from biting your nuts off." His laugh echoed in the parking lot. He turned away and went in a door two units down. They could hear him say as he went in, "Hey Mark, you're not going to believe who …" The door slammed shut. There was a loud whoop and then nothing.

Claudie watched Dwight and Sprocket as they talked quietly by the door. They were nervous, Dwight more fidgety than before.

There was a ping, a text message on Claudie's phone and Dwight scooped up the phone and read.

"Finally. He says it's too dark to find the money; he needs daylight. He'll meet us at the cabin at eight." Dwight looked over to Claudie, "You better hope he's on the up and up. He pulls any funny business there's going to be two unmarked graves out back of that cabin."

Claudie didn't bother to respond. Tomorrow was going to be an interesting day. She didn't know Dani well, but she was sure these jerks were going to be in for a life-changing surprise.

Chapter Nineteen

Saturday early morning

"Let's get this rodeo on the road, Professor." Nathan jerked up and looked out the rear view window of the silver Honda. It was still dark and he'd only had about three hours of sleep since Dani had retrieved the Dodge from the back lot of a car repair shop in Brookings. She'd slept in the Dodge after they had talked for about an hour about strategy. Their plan was still sketchy. He'd drive to the cabin in the Honda and meet the men holding Claudie. Dani would hide the Dodge up the road from the driveway and hike back. She'd hide near enough to make sure the exchange went smoothly. Any sign the men were going to renege, hurt Claudie or Nathan, then she was going to swoop down like an avenging angel. Her words. Her female warrior persona had always made Nathan smile. The comforting thing was that it wasn't bullshit. Anyone who'd ever messed with Dani had lived to regret it.

She followed him in the Charger to the driveway of the cabin and then continued down the road as he pulled in. The sky was just getting pale grey as he parked the car in front of the cabin next to the RV. He started to get out and then thought better of it. He turned the car back on and turned it so it was facing down the driveway. Quick get-away 101.

He sat and drank the now cold coffee that they had brought along. Dani joined him within twenty minutes. It was now half past six. They both knew that the men could be coming early, planning on their own welcoming committee. They hiked up to the meadow and looked under the water trough. The black plastic garbage bag was still sitting there and it didn't smell any better than Nathan remembered.

Dani circled the cabin, went inside, and looked around. She called for Nathan. Nathan came in and found her kneeling by the wretched heap that was Hammer.

"Is he alive?"

"Barely. Tommy did a bang-up job of fucking him over. He needs to get to hospital."

"Tommy one of your new friends?"

"He's a nasty piece of work is all I'll say. Here, help me prop him up. He'll breathe easier." They pulled him to a sitting position and leaned him against the wall.

They debated whether she should hide in the cabin or the RV. She decided on the RV. The keys had been left in it and it could prove to be another escape vehicle. Dani had a Beretta plus Claudie's Smith & Wesson. Nathan belatedly remembered his gun and retrieved it from under the sink. The small Sig Sauer fit nicely in the small of his back, under his shirt. He was still wearing the Brooks Brothers dress shirt he'd borrowed for the rehearsal dinner. Then he waited on the cabin's old porch, wondering how Claudie was holding up. She'd certainly gotten more than she bargained for since she'd invited him to join her for dinner. He wanted to make sure, after it was all over, that she felt it was worth it.

"We don't have time for that shit, Sprocket. I want to get to the cabin before the Professor does."

"I don't understand why she doesn't call me back. I've got the fucking dog. It's what she wanted." Sprocket went back into the room for Claudie.

"Keep that bastard on a tight leash. If he bites me he's going to get his hide peeled off." Sprocket was in an ugly mood and Claudie had no doubt he'd hurt the dog if things didn't go the way he hoped.

Claudie hesitated at the car door. Buddy did not want to get in the car. She had to get in first before the dog reluctantly followed. It was still dark. The neon light that had illumi-nated the parking lot was turned off and it seemed eerily deserted in the morning fog. Dwight started the car and in the sudden glare of the headlights they could see a guy slouched against a Coke machine, smoking a cigarette. Dwight backed the car out and turned south on Highway 101. The sky in the east above the coast range was pale. In the west one last star flickered on the horizon. They sped out of Gold Beach, Claudie hugged Buddy close for warmth and wearily watched the ocean's choppy waves. If the men kept their word, she could be free in a couple of hours. Now all she had to do was make sure that Buddy came with her, not handed over to Sprocket's dim-witted girlfriend.

When they passed the trailhead in the Pistol River area there was one lone highway patrol car parked at the side of the road. Claudie could see two officers in it but they didn't seem to pay any attention to the Malibu.

The birds were getting raucous as the light grew stronger, Nathan could hear crows and a few Stellar Jays. He heard the rumble of a motorcycle coming up the driveway. He scrambled to get into the cabin, tripping up the rotten wooden steps. He stood back from the door as the bike raced in and around to the back of the cabin. Sudden silence as the bike was turned off, and then Nathan could hear the biker cursing at his phone as he came around front. He held it up in the air and turned in a circle, trying to pick up a signal. He stood by the RV for several minutes and then at the sound of a car coming up the drive he climbed into the RV. Nathan watched anxiously. He blinked when he saw it rock a bit but it was silent when the red Malibu pulled up nose to nose with his Honda. So much for quick get-away 101.

Nathan watched from the cabin doorway as the driver got out. He was tall and skinny, not at all like Hammer or the passenger who opened his door. He recognized the ginger hair on a round head perched directly on the man's shoulders—Sprocket, Hammer's brother, the cretin from the campground. Nathan could see Claudie in the back seat but Sprocket leaned against her door so she couldn't get out. Nathan stepped out and stood on the second step, bouncing a little on his toes.

"Howdy, you must be the Professor. Quite the little stunt you pulled yesterday. Nearly got my cousin killed."

"I think what nearly got Hammer killed was the over-whelming stupidity of stealing a shipment of marijuana and trying to unload it in another gang's territory."

Sprocket moved toward Nathan, his hand reaching around to his back but the skinny man yelled at him to stop. He came to a halt three feet from the cabin steps and glared at Nathan. Nathan moved back to the top of the steps and smiled.

"Look, you've upset my other cousin. Sprocket, we need the nice Professor to tell us where the money is hidden. Then you can ask him for an apology. You'll apologize, won't you, Professor?"

"Certainly. Noblesse Oblige, etc." He was skating a fine line with these men. Angry men did stupid things. As Sun

Tzu said, "in the midst of chaos is opportunity." Not until Claudie was safe though could he unleash his pent-up fury at the men. He was gratified to notice that Claudie could now open her door if the opportunity arose.

"I didn't catch your name." Nathan attempted a more neutral tone to his voice. He already figured he was talking to Dwight, the mastermind of this entire imbroglio.

"Not important. I don't like to draw attention to myself. Now, do you want to tell me where you put my money?"

"I'd love to. The thing is, I spilled the motorcycle I escaped on yesterday and hit my head. My memory's a little hazy. Maybe if you let Claudie out of the car it would jog it a bit."

"You asshole, I'll jog your memory for you." Sprocket charged up the steps and on the second step, the spongy one, his foot crashed through the rotten wood and his leg was jammed into the jagged wood. He went down hard on his other knee and nearly did a face plant onto the steps. Nathan hopped back away from his flailing arms. Sprocket's face was a mural of pain and fury, and the cursing was thunderous. The skinny man cursed too, but it was directed at his cousin. He walked over to Sprocket and pulled the Glock out from the back of his pants. He aimed it at Nathan.

"Was that luck, Professor, or were you being clever?"

Nathan shrugged. They watched as Sprocket tried to extricate his leg from the broken step, but every move he made appeared to wedge his leg in ever more painful ways.

"Well, this could take all day. Have you by any chance

recovered your memory? Or, am I going to have to hurt your little girlfriend … oh, *fucking hell*!" He had turned to the Malibu to find that the rear passenger door was open and there was no sign of Claudie or the dog.

Good girl, Claudie. He'd caught a glimpse of her running toward the side of the cabin. One less thing to worry about. Now if Dani played her part, this little play could come to an end. Preferably before any more bikers showed up. But it was like merely thinking about them conjured them up. Both men could hear the roar of motorcycles flying up the driveway. Nathan ran to the far end of the porch and jumped off. He ran to the back, no sign of Claudie. She must have high-tailed it to the trees. A shot rang out and a bullet burrowed into the dirt to the right of him.

"Uh, uh, Professor. You have no intention of having the shit beat out of me like Hammer for information I don't have. You're going to be my 'get out of jail free' card. Let's take a little jog." Dwight waved the gun at Nathan, directing him toward the meadow. They could hear loud voices out front, Sprocket's not least among them. They got to the metal water trough and Dwight pointed the gun at the trough and said, "Sit." He crouched behind Nathan and they waited for the bikers to come looking for them.

"You got a plan, Moe?"

"Moe?"

"Certainly, You're Moe, the smart one, that's all relative, you know. Curly's out front, the one who has his foot stuck, metaphorically speaking, up his ass, and Larry, AKA Hammer, is the half-dead lump of shit in the cabin. The one you couldn't be bothered to take to the hospital."

"Christ. Hammer should have shot you when he had the chance."

"The world is full of lost opportunities, don't you think? So, smart guy, what's your plan?"

"Surprise, asshole. I get the drop on them and *pow*, I'm out of here with the cash."

"Hmmm. As Sun Tzu said in the Art of War, 'tactics without strategy is the noise before defeat'."

"Shut the fuck up." Dwight ducked down.

Two leather-clad bikers, with long stringy hair pulled back into ponytails, came around the house and stopped when they saw Nathan sitting calmly on the trough.

"Good morning, boys." Nathan projected an almost jolly welcome in his greeting. He added a jaunty little wave. He thought the look of bafflement on their stubbled faces was highly amusing. He stopped himself from laughing. It would have been impolitic. He heard Dwight curse softly. Good, now he had everybody left footed. If he could only figure out a way to not be in the middle of a gun battle.

"How can I help you?"

"Tell us where the other guy is. We need to talk to him about something."

"You didn't see him out front? He was carrying a big plastic sack full of money? He didn't sound like he was going to hang around."

"Oh yeah? The bozo with his foot trapped on the steps? He says his cousin ran this way." The biker looked around the meadow and then toward the trees. He nodded to the other man who hustled over to the deer path and disappeared into the trees. Nathan winced. He hoped that Claudie was working her way around front to the road.

"Boy, you had us all fooled last night. We thought you were just some dumb old man." The biker was the short one that Nathan had seen yesterday, the one called Mark who seemed to pull the most weight. He was grinning, but all the time his eyes were scanning the meadow, searching for any other surprises. Nathan could now see that he was holding a gun against his leg. Nathan hoped that Dani would spring her surprise soon.

"You got a gun, Professor? I thought I heard a shot when we came in."

"Nope, no gun. It must have been a backfire."

"Ain't no other cars around. I was wondering because one of my buddies was going to meet us here and I see his bike there but I don't see him."

"You know, I did hear a motorcycle earlier, I thought it went on by. Well, he'll show up soon, I'm sure." Behind the biker, on the far side of the house, Nathan caught a flash as Dani raced to the fence and hopped into the woods. Good, she'd protect Claudie. Now all he had to do was keep this yahoo distracted.

"Yeah? How come I think you're bullshitting me, Professor? You know, I bet your friend ain't huffing it down no forest path with a sack of money. That much money, it weighs a ton. For all I know you're sitting on top of the money you hid." The biker grinned and started to walk toward him.

Nathan stood and put his hand behind his back. The gun would have been more reassuring if he wasn't worried that Dwight could easily shoot him in the back. The biker stopped, his grin fading to a hard glare. His arm came up with his gun.

"Thought you said you didn't have a gun. You lie to me, Professor?"

Nathan smiled and shrugged.

"That half-dead loser in the cabin, the one Tommy performed an enhanced interrogation on? You fooled him good. He thought you were some old teacher who couldn't find his way out of a toilet stall. I never seen a dude as surprised as him when he realized the money was gone, and there was only one guy who could have stolen it. You get a laugh out of that, Professor?"

"Let's be honest. Fooling that moron didn't take a Ph.D. As the great Chinese general Sun Tzu said in the Art of War, 'Appear weak when you are strong, and strong when you are weak'."

"Huh." The biker smiled again. "What are you now, Professor? If you really have a gun behind your back, you could be strong. On the other hand, if you're bullshitting me, then you're in a pretty weak position. When Tommy gets back …"

Two gunshots rang out. The biker crouched down and looked toward the trees. Nathan, his heart thundering against his ribs, stepped away from the trough and pulled his gun out. He could see Dwight now. He was lying on his stomach staring into the woods. It took him a minute to realize that Nathan had moved. He twisted his head around, but he was in an awkward position. To face Nathan, he would expose himself to the biker. And he could see the gun in Nathan's hand. His face twisted in anger but he stayed silent.

The biker took in Nathan's change of position. If he felt threatened, he didn't show it. "Now you appear strong, Professor. Does that mean you're really weak? You even know how to fire that pea shooter?"

"I can hit a barn." Nathan smiled; he hoped it looked menacing.

"Maybe Tommy found your friend. Maybe he's going to come back with a sack of money and then we're going to leave you with your pals. I think they're going to be real unhappy with you. Of course, if Tommy doesn't have the sack and the money, we'll have to continue this negotiation."

"Sure taking Tommy a long time to come back from that forest path. Maybe he was shooting at a bear. Or, suppose he found a road or something? Maybe he's hiking down a timber road right now with the sack of money and no intention of coming back to split it with you."

The biker spit and looked into the trees, his head cocked

slightly, listening. Nathan shifted his gun toward the trough. He'd be able to at least disable Dwight; he was an easy enough target there on the ground. The wind rustled the treetops, but otherwise it was quiet. Not even the birds were twittering.

"Kind of like a Mexican standoff, don't you think?"

"Not quite. Looks like we got another guest to the party. That your old lady, Professor? Not bad looking for an old broad, I think she makes a good negotiating chip, don't ya' think?"

Nathan looked toward the trees with a sinking heart. Claudie was standing in the path with her hands held high. From where she stood she could see them and also Dwight behind the trough. He couldn't see Dani.

"Tommy?"

Claudie looked behind herself and then back at the biker. "He was having trouble with the sack. It started to rip."

"Jesus. Come on over here where I can keep an eye on you."

Claudie hesitantly walked toward the biker, her hands high and a look of fear on her face. She stopped about ten feet on the far side of him and collapsed into a trembling pile. She started to cry. Gut wrenching wails filled the meadow.

"He shot my dog. My poor little dog." She sobbed, her arms beating the ground.

"Oh, for Christ's sake." The biker turned his attention back to Nathan and the deer path.

Without a pause in her wailing, Claudie reached around

and pulled her Smith & Wesson out of her pants and shot at the biker's chest. Bright red holes peppered his chest; he twisted toward her in shock before sinking to the ground. She dropped her gun, her face mirroring the biker's shock. Dani came out of the woods and went over to the biker. She picked up his gun and walked over to Claudie.

"Relax. You have scattershot in your gun remember. All you did was surprise him." She placed an arm around Claudie, who exhaled a long held breath. "Good job. You played hysterical old lady like a pro."

Nathan now turned his gun on Dwight, who was crawling around the trough; he put a bullet in the dirt by his head.

"Drop the gun, Dwight, and stand up. Dani, the biker in the woods?"

"No hurry. Tommy's not going anywhere."

"Thanks." For all her bravado, Claudie suddenly leaned against the cabin and wrapped her arms around herself.

Nathan started to go to her, his attention to Dwight wavered and Dwight took advantage of Nathan's distraction. He picked up his gun and raised it toward Nathan. Nathan beat him by two nanoseconds. He only winged him, but Dwight dropped the gun. He clutched his upper arm as blood leaked through his fingers and down his shirt.

"Holy crap. I'm beginning to feel like a fifth wheel. Aren't you two pros?" Dani walked over to Nathan and whispered, "You might want to see to Claudie—she's more rattled than she wants to let on."

Nathan hurried over to Claudie and without saying a word enveloped her in his arms and held her tight. She was trembling and breathing deep and fast.

"I am so sorry about Buddy. He was a nice dog ..."

Claudie twisted out of his arms, "Oh, hell. I forgot him. I tied him up to a tree."

Nathan followed her a short way up the deer path. Buddy started barking and leaping around when he caught sight of Claudie. His leash was looped around a dead branch of a fallen tree. Before Claudie could reach him there was a loud crack and the branch broke off. Buddy came bounding toward them, dragging a four-foot dead branch. It was a crazy dance as Nathan tried to unleash the dog from the branch without getting thwacked by it, and Claudie tried to keep Buddy from knocking her over. They all ended up sitting on the ground while Buddy licked first one face then the other. Claudie started laughing.

"Buddy, let me get a shot at this." Nathan leaned past the dog and, cupping Claudie's face, planted a long emphatic kiss. "I'm so glad you're safe. I was so worried."

Claudie took a big shuddering breath. "It was your turn. I've been worried sick about you for days."

Chapter Twenty

Claudie and Nathan helped each other to their feet and headed back to the cabin. Mark was still lying on the ground, alive, but Dani had wrapped his arms and legs with duct tape. She had Dwight sitting on the porch next to Sprocket. Dwight held a hand to his useless arm; the bleeding had slowed to a trickle. He'd live.

"Okay, guys. We've got to decide how to deal with these jokers." Dani leaned against the Honda, one hand holding her Beretta steady at the two cousins.

"I can go call the police and we can …"

"Oh, no. That won't work."

"Nathan, you want to explain the problem to her?"

"Claudie, Dani doesn't like to interact with the authorities. We need to come up with a plan or story that keeps her out of this."

"But we've got to call the police. And Hammer needs to get to a hospital. You said he was dying."

"What the fuck, Dwight? Hammer is dying? You said he was okay." Sprocket was clearly not happy with this news.

"Jesus Spock, I'm not a doctor. He seemed fine to me."

"You couldn't even take the time to take him to a hospital. You were so obsessed with the money you left Hammer alone to die in this shitty cabin."

"He ain't dead yet. You need to calm down, Spock ..."

"Stop calling me Spock." Sprocket screamed and lunged at Dwight. Too late Dwight realized that he'd poked the bear one time too many. He tried to roll away but Sprocket grabbed his legs and pulled him back. Then, before Nathan or Dani could do anything, those giant mitts closed around Dwight's throat and did not let go. Dwight thrashed around, his one good hand clawing at Sprocket's death grip. A shot rang out; Dani put a bullet in the porch just to the right of Sprocket's head. He let go, and Dwight rocked back and forth, his face bright red and his mouth sucking for air.

Sprocket started to do a crazy combination of laughing and crying. Nathan and Claudie stood in stunned silence.

"We've got a lot of loose ends going on here, guys." Dani laid Mark's gun on the Honda's trunk. Beside it she put Nathan's Glock that she had retrieved from Dwight and next to it Claudie's Smith & Wesson.

"I'd say that's a grand understatement. As Sun Tzu said ..."

"Please don't, Nathan. Unless Sun Tzu had a jiffy suggestion on how to get rid of all these bodies, I don't want to hear it."

"Fine. I think he burned a lot of ..."

"*No!* Are you crazy? You'd start a forest fire." Nathan and Dani had forgotten Claudie in the excitement. She continued, "Why can't Nathan and I call the police? We can blame everything on the bikers. Drug deal gone wrong."

"That's the angle I vote for. Except the part where you call the police. Claudie, do you really want to go through an inquest? Let me ask you one question that a prosecutor is going to home in on. Were you in immediate bodily danger when you shot that biker? The answer is no."

"But I thought he was going to shoot Nathan. I thought you said he wasn't dead."

"Not yet. At the least, you'll be charged with reckless endangerment, maybe manslaughter if he doesn't make it. You're looking at a long, expensive trial. And the press will go through every dirty tidbit of your life. And Nathan, his quiet life will be destroyed too. That what you want?"

Claudie shook her head. Nathan put his arm around her and held her tight.

"We got one other problem." Dani looked at Sprocket and Dwight. "What about them?"

Sprocket was still sobbing into his hands and didn't look up. He had finally pulled his leg out of the wooden step.

"Let's start with what the police do know. The marijuana was stolen in Merlin." Nathan paused in thought. "But they've been so distracted by the biker rally they haven't had time to concentrate on it. An anonymous tip could point them in this direction. When they finally come up here they'll find these jokers and the bodies. It'll look like what it was, a shoot-out over the drugs and money. They'll wrap up the case with that. The Oregon State Police are too under-funded to dig deeper."

"You think those idiots will forget about you?" Dani waved her Beretta at Sprocket and Dwight.

"Oh no, Dani. No more killing." Nathan reached over and put a restraining hand on her arm. She frowned and shook it off.

"They're loose ends, Nathan. They've seen us all, and they've probably heard our names. I, for one, don't want to worry that they'll say the wrong thing to the wrong people."

"Then make sure they don't talk, Dani. You've guaranteed the silence of smarter people than these morons. Give them the come-to-Jesus talk. Give them a cast iron reason to not open their mouths."

Dani stared at the heaving sack of misery that was Sprocket Head. He had crawled into the cabin and from the sound of his wail they knew that Hammer had at last met his maker. He slumped in the cabin doorway, his pant leg was ripped and bloody, and his tee-shirt had streaks of blood, not all his. He looked up at Dani and said, "Go ahead and shoot. I ain't got nothing to live for." Defeat was writ large across his heavy face.

"Okay, here, have at it. Shoot yourself, in the mouth works best." Dani handed him Mark's gun. "No, wait, that's out of bullets. Here." She grabbed it back and gave him her Beretta. Nathan and Claudie shouted as Sprocket took the gun and without a pause put it in his mouth and pulled the trigger. Click. Click. Click. He took it out and tossed it to Dani, total disgust on his face.

"Fucking bitch."

Dani picked up the gun with a tissue and laid it on the trunk of the Honda next to Mark's gun.

"Here's how it's going to go, Sprocket. We have two murder weapons. They both have your fingerprints on them. I don't care where you go, but it has to be far away. Mexico would be good. Alaska if you don't like the heat. You never saw me or my friends. You never come near any of us. If you even think about us, if you get drunk and start talking about us, I will see that this gun ends up in the hands of the police with a nice little story about how you murdered your brother, cousin, and the three bikers. Do you understand? Say yes, I understand."

Sprocket mumbled the words.

"Good. Now, you stay put." She turned her attention to Dwight and frowned. Dwight had stopped thrashing. In fact, it appeared that he had stopped breathing too, his hands were clutching his throat and his face was blue.

Dani went over and put a hand on his throat. "Shit, his windpipe's crushed. Guess we won't have to worry about this sucker."

"This is insane. Are you going to let a murderer go? Do you really think this will work?" Claudie looked at Nathan.

"Dani has spooked scarier characters than that sad sack. As for murder, his brother just died, probably might have lived if Dwight had taken him to a hospital. I'm sure a good defense lawyer would get him off." He looked over at Sprocket and then motioned Dani over to the RV doorway. "What am I going to find inside my RV?"

"The biker in your RV. Sorry. He's not a problem. That one is a friend. Kind of. Help me get him out." Dani handed Claudie back her gun and then ducked into the RV with Nathan. Inside, Zach was bound with the ubiquitous duct tape. He was conscious and deeply unhappy.

"We need to move him into the cabin. He's going to be the one to help make this mess go away."

"Should I ask how?"

"No."

"Why was the dog so important, Sprocket?" Claudie could almost feel pity for the poor schmuck. Then she remembered him trying to break her car window to get Buddy.

Sprocket chuffed some air. "Aileen wanted him back. She took my truck."

"Maybe you can get her another dog."

"Nah. Fuck her. I'm getting the hell out like that lady said."

Claudie heard a couple of thumps behind her and turned to see Dani step out of the RV. She was manhandling a bound man out of the RV. She pushed him up the steps to the cabin.

"Jesus. That's one scary bitch."

"Yep. I wouldn't want to be on her bad side either."

A few minutes later, Nathan and Dani disappeared around the side of the cabin. They returned dragging a black plastic sack. They hauled it into the RV.

"Oh man, the money." Sprocket groaned in disgust.

Dani came out and tossed a small roll of money at Sprocket. "Travel money. You're going to get into the Malibu. When you get to Highway 101 you go north or south, I don't care, but don't stop."

She turned back to Nathan and Claudie. "You guys sure you didn't drop anything? Don't want to leave any confusing evidence for the cops."

"Are we going to leave the bodies where they are now?"

"Pretty much. You never want to leave a crime scene looking like it was staged. Murder au naturel is best. You guys take off—you got a wedding to go to after all. I'll meet you later as soon as I know this buffoon is making the right choice."

"What about the police?"

"I'll phone it in later, Claudie. Stop obsessing."

Nathan started the RV and Claudie cleared the garbage out of the passenger seat. She let Buddy in first and then climbed in. The RV smelled like a dirty tavern: beer, urine, and shit.

Claudie rolled down her window and watched the green trees rush by her window.

"I can't believe what just happened. It's like a nightmare, only real. I don't think I'm ever going to get this out of my mind. I shot a man today."

"You shot a dangerous man who meant us harm. If you'd seen what they did to Hammer, you wouldn't feel so bad."

She shuddered. It was surreal. In an hour they'd be at King Wesley's beautiful house and Nathan would watch his lovely niece get married. All she wanted to do was crawl in bed and sleep. But not to dream. Not to dream for a long time.

Chapter Twenty-One

Saturday afternoon

"Let's stop here, I'm starved. And I don't know if I'm ready to face the Wesleys." Claudie pointed at Barnacle Bistro and Nathan drove the RV around to a side street to park.

"Good old Barnacles. I've had their fish and chips going on twenty years."

"I thought they were good." Claudie paused before opening the door. "Will it bring back sad memories?"

"No. My memories of Kay are happy. And after the last few days, I've decided to pursue new happy ones. Something about almost being killed focuses the mind on living."

"My thoughts exactly. I know it's a cliché but it's true. And frankly? I don't think I have a lot of time to screw around anymore. There's so much I want to see and do."

"I agree. Except you have one thing wrong. We've spent the last few days with people who've made us feel old and useless. They are wrong, dead wrong if you will excuse a bad pun. We are not old, Claudie. We are … well-seasoned."

Claudie laughed long and hard, then leaned over and gave Nathan a kiss. It wasn't an old crone's kind of kiss. Buddy tried to get in on the act but they pushed him down.

"Look! There's a bunch of people parasailing. Now that would be fun. What do …"

"Nope, not going to happen. Scared of heights." Claudie got out of the RV and they stood for a few moments watching brightly colored parasails swoop over the water and beach.

They took their time at lunch then they drove up to King's to find the driveway full of caterer and floral vans. With a little bit of coaxing they were able to get a couple of the vans moved so Nathan could park down the little drive to the horse trailer.

"I'm going up to the house and see what's going on, want to come?"

"No. I crave peace and quiet. I'm going to sit and look at the ocean. After that huge lunch, I'll probably fall asleep inside ten minutes."

Nathan disappeared up the drive and Claudie plopped down on the lounge chair. The parasailers were still out over the beach and she watched them for the eight and a half minutes she could keep her eyes open.

"Uncle Nathan! Where have you been? Daddy wanted you to go parasailing with us. He's very put out." Ellie was sitting in a little side patio watching the backyard being transformed into the set of Midsummer Night's Eve.

"That's his natural state with me, Ellie. You look bewitching."

"I look a mess! I went out first thing and my hair is a complete rat's nest. Mother is quite put out about the whole thing."

"That's her natural state too. Is there anything I can do to help with this circus?"

"No. Mother's harassing the caterers. And Ginger, Eric's mom, she's in charge of making the florist miserable. I'm free till Daddy gets back. He and Eric are still sailing around. I do hope I don't become a widow before I'm even married. You know how Daddy gets."

"Yes. The energizer bunny can get quite competitive. He probably wants to show everybody that he can keep up with his new son-in-law." Nathan sat on a cast iron chair and looked at his favorite niece. She was like a daughter without the issues.

"That's probably why Daddy has trouble with you."

"Why's that?"

"You don't play his games. He thinks you're just some ole

boring philosophy professor. He thought Aunt Kay must have been bored to tears. But I know better."

"Do you?"

"I saw you in Rome, remember? You and Aunt Kay did everything. You traveled, you went to archeology digs, you went on a safari. Ha! Daddy couldn't believe you went to darkest Africa and didn't kill anything. He didn't see the point. He just doesn't get you. What I don't understand is how you've settled down in Sisters for so long. Aren't you bored?"

"No, I'm not. It's a lovely town, with lively people who have incredible life stories. They come into the bookstore and talk about their lives, the books they like, the places they want to go someday. I've already been to a lot of those places. I like my life now and my friends."

"Like your friend Claudie? I bet there's some stories in her past."

"Why do you say that?"

"I googled her. She has a blog. She doesn't write about dramatic stuff, but little everyday stuff that she makes so funny. And she's dropped a few hints. I think she's been married a few times. You must bring her to the wedding tonight. Wait here, I found something for her." Ellie disappeared into the house and Nathan watched the melee out in the garden.

"What's that?" Claudie squinted in the late afternoon light. Nathan was holding up a midnight blue silk dress. It didn't look like it would fit him.

"Your dress for the wedding, madam. Ellie insists you accompany me and you know it's bad luck to disappoint a bride-to-be."

"She's milking that bride thing real hard."

"Oh yeah. She's more like King than she'd ever admit. I still like her. And I'd like you to be with me when she gets married. I may get very emotional and I'll need your support."

Claudie laughed. "Fine. But if you get weepy, bring a handkerchief. You can't cry on that silk, you'd ruin it. Where'd she get it? It's not her size."

"Probably from her mother's back closet."

"That's going to make me popular with Mrs. W. You know, it's funny. That woman didn't like me on sight. Usually I have to open my mouth before people hate me."

"She doesn't like competition. You are entirely too attractive and intelligent for her."

Claudie's face got warm. "That's nice of you to say. Just because I saved your life you really don't need to …" Nathan cut her off with a kiss. Breaking it off, Claudie said, "I need more than a dress to make my entrance at this wedding. I need a shower. Something has to happen to my hair, and shoes! I need shoes. I can't go in hiking shoes."

Nathan shook a paper bag he'd dropped by her chair. Everything you need's in here. Including 'The Wiz', King's Supreme all-in-one deluxe grooming tool. The only grooming aid you'll ever need rolled into one."

Claudie looked in the bag and pulled out the giant red plastic tool. "I tried this the other day. I couldn't figure it out."

"I know. You need a training manual the size of the New American Webster's Dictionary. Let me show you. Now, here's the little part I like the best." He pried a small cylindrical tube from the base.

"I'm stumped. What is it?"

"Nose hair trimmer. Ears too but I haven't had to go there yet."

"Good to know. Anything for chinny chin hairs?"

"Absolutely. Electric clippers or, right here, tweezers."

"Cool. Now show me how you turn the blow dryer on."

Nathan plugged it into the outdoor extension cord for the lamp and began pressing and twisting.

"I didn't mean for it to be an intelligence test."

Nathan laughed. "It's a bit like a Rubik's cube. Give me a sec."

Claudie waited, her smile getting broader and broader. Finally the blower started with a roar and Nathan waved it triumphantly.

"Shall we go and get cleaned up?"

"Together? Now that would piss off Mrs. W." Claudie's eyes sparkled at the thought.

"Enticing, but for propriety's sake we should probably shower separately."

"Fine, I get dibs first."

"Of course."

Chapter Twenty-Two

Saturday afternoon

"You gonna shoot me now that the Professor and old lady are gone?" Sprocket stared down at Hammer's body.

"No, I'll keep my word. Get in the car." Dani waved her gun at him for encouragement.

"It don't seem right leaving Hammer here like this."

"The dead don't care anymore. The county will bury him and you can always say a prayer or something when you go to bed tonight. Commend him to god, or in his case, more likely Satan."

Sprocket sighed and started the Malibu. He backed up and

drove down the driveway thinking of where he wanted to go. There was always the chance that he could get his truck back from Aileen. Without the dog it would be a hard sell. The thought of Mexico didn't appeal to him since he didn't know the lingo. He liked that TV program about Alaska. Maybe he'd go north and work on a fishing boat or something. At Highway 101 he turned right and headed toward Gold Beach. His leg was hurting awfully bad and he thought he might stop at a doctor's to get a shot or something. Some oxy would be nice. He pulled over to the side of the road as he neared the Pistol River area. The motorcycles whizzing by made him nervous, but he needed to see if he could get Aileen on the phone. His call went to voicemail and he left another message. He wondered what would happen if he walked down to the beach and looked for her but the thought of all the bikers there scared the shit out of him. He started the car up and drove on to Gold Beach.

He found an urgent care clinic and pulled into the parking lot but it was full. On a side street he found a space and started to limp back to the clinic. And there, in plain sight on the street, was his pick-up, the truck bed empty except for sand and pine needles. He looked around but no sign of Aileen or where she could be. He hobbled to the clinic's door and went inside. And froze in place. Every seat in the waiting room was occupied by leather-clad men and tattooed women. There were bloody and bruised faces, broken arms clutched to people's chests, and not a piece of clothing that didn't looked ripped and filthy. The moaning was low and constant and kinda creepy, Sprocket thought. If he waited here it would be hours before a doctor could see him. Not worth it.

He turned to go when he heard, "Sprocket, honey."

Aileen grabbed his arm and spun him back. He caught a glimpse of a tear stained face sporting an enormous black eye before she attached herself to his chest and held on for dear life.

"Aileen. What happened?"

She started crying and Sprocket looked around for help. No one paid any attention to them.

"Come outside and talk to me. There ain't no room in here." He pulled her out to the parking lot.

"Did that guy hit you? If he punched you I'm going to …"

"No, no. It wasn't him. It was the bitch he was screwing in *my* tent. He sent me out for more beer and when I came back he had some biker chick in our tent. I got a little mad, I guess. I started to whale on her and she started screaming and punching and the next thing you know some biker climbs in and starts hitting Oleg and then it got really nasty. The tent fell down and I don't think anyone knew who they was hitting. I was lucky. I got out of the tent first and then the biker dude came out, dragging the chick, and Oleg was lying all tangled in the tent screaming like a banshee. His arm is broke for sure, and maybe some ribs. I don't know, and I don't care. I brought him here and all I want to do is get the hell out. Will you help me, Sprocket? I could always depend on you and I was just plain dumb to leave you like that. Can you forgive me?"

Sprocket looked down on her dirty blonde head and felt a tsunami of love and relief. He had his girl back. Now, if he only had some cash they could go to Alaska and he could buy her one of them huskies and live on a boat. But this time he was going to be the one in charge. He wasn't going to let her run all over him like before.

"I seen my truck there. Where's the dope, Aileen? You want me to forgive you, I can do that, but I need the dope. We can use the money to settle down someplace. Live like normal people, you know."

"What about Hammer and your cousin? Won't they take all the money? Hammer's always making you do things you oughtn't and ..."

"Hammer ain't going to mess with us anymore. He's ... he's ... he's dead." Sprocket started to bawl again.

"Oh, Sprocket baby. It'll be alright. I hid that dope in my grandma's garage in Grants Pass. We can go get it, deal a little to pick up some cash and then head out somewhere far away."

"You like boats?"

"Huh?"

"I was thinking about Alaska."

"I don't know. Alaska's awful cold."

"It's where I'm heading, Aileen." Sprocket's voice was strong and determined, and Aileen loved it.

"Then it's Alaska, honey pot."

They kissed and walked arm in arm back to the truck.

"Where's Jasper?"

Sprocket stopped and looked solemnly at her, "Jasper is in heaven, Aileen. It's a long story but he didn't suffer any."

Aileen's face crumpled a little but she handed him the keys to the truck and they got in. By the time they rolled into Grants Pass, the future looked bright and good to them both.

Dani watched Sprocket pull away in the Malibu. She picked up one of the splintered boards from the cabin steps and then walked around the cabin to where Mark was still lying in the dirt. He was still alive and she needed some information from him. She thought in his current position he might be easy to persuade. He opened his eyes when he heard her approach.

"I thought Zach dumped your sorry ass in Grants Pass."

"Hardly. Men don't leave me, not till I want them to."

"You look different. Sound different too. Lost the accent. You a cop?"

"No. You're going to wish I was a cop before I'm done with you. I'm not so nearly as delicate as your average cop. If you want to avoid a world of hurt you're going to tell me what I need to know."

"I'm already hurting, bitch." He laughed.

"Hardly. That was just scattershot. Poked a few little holes in you is all. No, I'm talking real pain. I've spent some time in Iraq and Syria. Those people know a thing or two about pain." She tapped the board against her leg.

His eyes narrowed. She could see his body tense, straining against the duct tape. But, it was futile. Dani brought the board down hard on his right knee and the clearing filled with his outraged howl.

Dani waited. "Come on, Mark. I don't like this any more than you do. We can end this now. There's a name I need. She leaned down and whispered something in his ears. Her phone was recording this exchange and she didn't want this on the video. She planned on giving the recording to Zach. It would give him some leverage with Mark.

"Jesus. I don't know."

She jabbed the splintered end down hard on the hand clutching his knee.

"I don't know. Jesus, please, I'm just a middle guy." Tears began to form in his eyes.

"Yeah. Middle management sucks, don't it? But I know you see stuff, hear stuff. I want to know everything."

An hour later, Dani went into the cabin to talk to Zach. She didn't cut the duct tape; he looked a little upset with her.

"That went well. I think I have what I needed."

"You just ruined a federal investigation because of what? You've never even told me what you're up to. What ever it is, when I'm done with you …"

"You're going to thank me is what you're going to do. All you want is the big flashy bust, guns, and drugs. Make the taxpayers think they're getting what they paid for."

"Who do you work for?"

"Myself. I'm a free agent and I help who I please. The little guys who you ATF and FBI guys can't be bothered with."

"Tommy was right. You're a fucking angel of mercy."

"Don't make me hurt you, Zach. I'm going to leave now." She set a pocketknife down on the floor.

"When you get yourself cut loose you'll find Mark out back in a very cooperative mood. You can make him a class A informant. If he gets out of line, remind him I recorded our little talk on my phone. I'll send you a copy. I told him if he got out line I'd send the video to certain persons who will not be as gentle with him as I was."

Zach snorted.

"That's okay. Thank me later after your press conference crowing how you saved Americans from their own foolish fascination with guns and dope."

"I don't see you laying down your arms."

"No. I'm a hypocrite like everybody else. One day I'll buy a little tropical island, live there with no other people. Maybe then I'll feel safe."

She walked to the door. "It would probably be best if you didn't speak about me to any of your colleagues. What happened here was a drug deal gone bad. Without Tommy, you're now the number two bad guy. Congratulations."

Chapter Twenty-Three

Saturday night

Claudie felt conspicuous as Nathan guided her to the second row of seats. The minister, she was disappointed to see, did not have a colander on his head, and the flowers were soft peach; there was not a string of pasta to be seen. The groom looked confident and his groomsmen looked sunburned and jovial. The pianist was playing something sedate and the other guests gossiped and strained their necks to see what other people were wearing, and who was with whom.

"King wanted Eric to fly in on a gyrocopter but Ellie put her foot down."

"I'm sure it would have given Mrs. W a heart attack. The ladies' hats would have been flying all over the place." She stopped whispering as Mrs. W was escorted to her seat directly in front of her. Mrs. W was in a pale blue fitted dress that showed where Ellie got her fine figure. The wedding march began and they all turned in their seats to watch as King walked his daughter down the aisle. Ellie was wearing a simple, palest yellow, satin silk gown with a deep V in the back. She was beautiful and Eric's eyes shone brightly as his bride approached. King handed off his only daughter and joined Mrs. W, who was holding a handkerchief to her mouth. The wedding ceremony was not terribly long. The bride and groom exchanged personal vows and with a kiss they were married.

When Mrs. W rose with King to follow them back down the aisle she glanced briefly at Claudie and Claudie caught a slight pursing of her lips. Claudie had no doubt that Mrs. W had recognized her dress. It was embarrassing but Claudie had suffered worse. She dearly hoped that she didn't spill anything on the damn thing. She thought she should probably not eat or drink anything. She smiled to herself, not going to happen. She'd seen the food the caterers had prepared and there was definitely some prime rib destined for her plate.

The picture taking took longer than the wedding ceremony and Claudie sipped good champagne and waited patiently at a reserved table. She was relieved that Nathan was not expected to sit in front with the other relatives. But as everyone sat down she found herself directly in front of Mrs. W again. There wasn't any escaping her baleful glances. Well, dearie, I've handled way worse than you this week. Ollie and Alvin were seated at the far end and Claudie could avoid looking at them and remembering the sounds from the other night. She hoped they'd be too tired for any hanky panky tonight.

After the dinner was served the band started to tune up. The first dance was a slow tune for the new bride and groom and the parents soon joined them on the dance floor. Next up was Alvin and Ollie, and Alvin showed the other men how good ballroom dancing was done.

"How are you holding up?"

"I'm trying not to think about how tired I am. This is good medicine to help me forget about what happened this morning. They look so happy. I hope they have a wonderful and long life together."

"I think they will. Ellie chose well. Eric has the same ideals. Did I tell you where they're going on their honeymoon?"

Claudie shook her head no.

"Haiti. They've volunteered for a month. Ellie is an ophthalmologist and Eric just finished dental school. Ellie keeps thinking that you're the surprise I said I was bringing but it's a donation."

"That's nice. What is it?"

"Some equipment for the clinic they'll work in. A Bend dentist was retiring and I bought some of his stuff. I had it shipped there last week. Hopefully it will help Eric and other volunteers who go down there."

"You know what? I think Ellie is a lucky girl to have you for her uncle. You are an incredibly thoughtful man."

Nathan shook his head slightly. "I just didn't think they needed another toaster. Do you want to dance? I'm not very good but I think I can manage a turn or two."

"I'd love to. I warn you, I haven't danced for a couple of years. And there's one thing I will not do."

Nathan looked at her questioningly.

"No twerking. Hurts my back."

"I know what you mean." He took her elbow and they went out to the dance floor. It was a long slow dance and at first Claudie felt stiff in Nathan's arms but when it ended, they waited for the next one. It was an old Jerome Kern melody, "The Way You Look Tonight", and she began to relax into Nathan's embrace. The band played one more romantic song before the beat picked up and the younger crowd started taking over from the older guests. Soon the only one over fifty on the dance floor was King. Nathan guided Claudie to a table on the edge of the lawn and then excused himself for a minute.

Claudie watched the young people; their enthusiasm exhilarated her. She felt younger than she had in years, not that she wanted to join them on the dance floor. But their energy was infectious and the dances with Nathan, the warmth and strength of his arms around her, stirred something deep. Something she thought she'd buried a long time ago. She shook her head with a rueful smile. She needed to stop this line of thinking. There was no way she'd ever expose herself like that again. It wasn't just in the physical sense, although getting naked at her age would take a whole lot more wine than she'd had so far. It was also in the emotional sense. But, some people started romances at her age. And maybe the optimism of the young people was wearing off on her. She remembered how it felt to kiss him—it felt good.

Nathan returned holding a cold bottle of Dom Perignon and two flutes.

"What say we ditch this joint? Let's move the party to someplace quieter and more scenic."

"Fine." She followed him toward the hedge separating the lawn from the little road to the trailer. As she slipped into the darkness she glanced back to see Ollie staring at them, her smile a broad indication of approval.

It was, of course, not any quieter on the little makeshift patio, but certainly less frenetic. The ambient light from the celebration made the stars dim and far between. They could faintly hear the surf down below. Nathan poured the champagne and they sat in silence for several minutes.

"There's one thing I've wanted to ask you."

"Which is?"

"The money. If you're not going to the police, are you planning on keeping the money?"

"Interesting question." Nathan paused. "I thought about giving a chunk to Ellie and Eric for the clinic. That would be a good use."

"Noble."

"It's not like I'd be stealing it from upstanding citizens. It's drug money. And they did cause me a lot of pain and suffering."

"So, it's like you sued them and won a big settlement?"

"It could be viewed that way."

"If the authorities question the guy who bought the dope, and then they look at what happened at the cabin, don't you think they'll wonder what happened to it?"

"I'm hoping they'll assume other bad guys took it."

Claudie nodded, "What if there *are* other bad guys and they know that the money is floating around somewhere. Aren't you afraid they'll come looking for it?"

"No. Dani said she'd leave a couple clues, dead ends, and misdirections for anyone who might become interested."

"So, Dani's in on this?"

"Finders fee, so to speak."

"Nice work if you can get it. Say, do I get a cut? I rode a horse to this rodeo."

"Absolutely. I was thinking twenty-five percent. Would you like that?"

"Who couldn't use a few hundred thousand dollars?" She started laughing so hard some champagne went up her nose. "Wow. I can't believe we're talking about this. This entire day, hell, the last three days have been surreal. Are you sure you're just a philosophy teacher?"

"As the great actor Liam Neeson said, 'I am a man with a particular skill set.' I'm very analytical. It's the training in logic, I guess. I discovered that I can track money, find where it's transferred, and who's hiding it. I know all the hidey-holes. I did consulting work for the government. The less said about that the better."

"Okay, I've got time to wheedle it out of you. I hope you know how to find a way for us deposit the money without undue attention from the government. Cause I think the Sisters' Community Bank might wonder where I found four hundred thousand dollars in cash. They might ask questions."

"I'd love to be your financial advisor. I was thinking we'd travel. We could scout out banks in the Cayman's. Cape Verde is a good place to park cash."

"Wait. How do 'we' get it there? Don't you think the airport security will have a lot of undesirable questions?"

"Private planes. Security is not the same."

"So that's how all those rich oligarchs do it."

"Very popular. Do you want some more champagne?"

"A little. I don't want to get sloppy."

"Who's going to know?"

"You. Another question."

"Okay."

"What's your opinion on elder sex? A wise old woman told me recently that it keeps you young. She also said if you don't use it, you lose it. And do you think we should worry about protection?"

Nathan looked at her, a smile growing wide on his face. "If it would make you feel better, I could go ask one of the young folks if they have a condom to spare."

Claudie snorted and stood up. "Don't you dare." She reached down and took his hand. They went into the trailer and shut the door. A great deal of laughter ensued and blended in with the merry making next door.

Dani stepped away from the RV and looked at the horse trailer. She could see it rocking a little and she grinned. Nathan, you old coot. Someone at last to make you happy. She put a box on the patio table and then pulled the black plastic sack after her as she disappeared up the drive.

Chapter Twenty-Four

Sunday morning

Bam, bam, bam. "Nathan, rise and shine. I got a boat chartered. Let's go fishing." King banged on the side of the trailer again.

"Go away, King. I'm busy." Nathan's muffled reply was accompanied by Claudie's stifled giggling.

"Mrs. King made us a lunch of leftovers from the wedding. She's not going to be happy about this."

"Don't tell her. It's none of her business. King, go play with someone else."

"Fine. Do you want me to take this box up and put it with Ellie's other gifts?"

"What box?" Nathan finally cracked the door and looked out. He was wearing boxers and the dress shirt from last night. On the patio was a box wrapped in silver paper. A little open card was attached, "To Ellie, love, Dani."

"Hmmm. I guess. I didn't realize she left something. Go ahead. Ellie and Eric are still here?"

"Yeah. I let them sleep in. They're going up to Portland later for their flight to Haiti." King looked Nathan up and down with a grin and craned his neck a little, trying to peek into the trailer. "I hope you had a good night's sleep."

"Best in years. Thanks. We'll be up later for breakfast."

"Mrs. King will love that. I might not hang around." He picked up the box and went back to the house.

Nathan went back inside the trailer and found the dog had replaced him on the bed.

"I guess Dani's come and gone."

"Do you think she …?"

"Not a lot gets by Dani. Let's get dressed and try to look respectable."

"Impossible for me. Mrs. W's had my number from the start."

Thirty minutes and many kisses later, the guilty couple walked into the kitchen. Mrs. W glanced up from her paper and then with a scowl went back to reading. Ollie looked up with a wicked grin. The silver box sat on the kitchen island next to Ellie who was sipping coffee and reading some of the gift cards. She turned and gave them a radiant and knowing smile.

King was putting the finishing touches on an impromptu buffet with leftovers from the wedding.

"Coffee's hot and I can whip you up some eggs and bacon if you'd like."

"Not for me. I'll nibble on this. What about you, Claudie?"

"This looks great. I've got a tea bag, can I boil some water?"

"Whatever you'd like. Anything for Nathan's girl."

Mrs. W grunted softly, but not too softly and slapped the newspaper down on the table. She opened her mouth to say something but Ellie's piercing squeal made everyone turn to her in alarm.

The silver box was open and Ellie was staring at the plastic wrapped bundle of money in her hand. "Uncle Nathan! I can't believe this. Look what Dani gave us. Where is she, I can't … I'm totally stunned. Eric! Eric! Come in here."

Eric walked in from another room and gaped at the money. "What the hell. Who's Dani? Did I meet her?"

"She's Uncle Nathan's friend. Where is she? I need to thank her. Honey, look. I think there's enough to fund the clinic for months. Uncle Nathan, did you know about this?"

Nathan shook his head and watched as Eric tore the plastic covering off and began to count.

"There's like two hundred thousand dollars here." Eric wrapped his arms around Ellie and they did a little dance.

King peeked into the box and then looked at the stack of

money. He thumbed the stack, "At least they're not sequential serial numbers. How are the kids going to explain two hundred thousand dollars in cash, Nathan?"

"I can probably help them out. There's always the Caymans. We can deposit the cash there and then the kids can send it wherever they'd like."

"Where are you going?" King shouted after Nathan as he hustled out of the kitchen, Claudie close on his heels.

"Where are you going, Nathan?" Claudie echoed King.

He didn't answer her. He tugged on the RV door, "This was locked last night." Claudie followed him in and watched as he flung back the mattress in the bedroom. There was nothing there. Nathan looked around wildly, running his hand through his hair. Claudie sat at the little table in the kitchenette and found a white envelope with Nathan's name on it.

"There's a letter."

Nathan tore the envelope open and extracted a sheet of paper. He read it quickly. He flung it down on the table and went into the small bathroom. Claudie picked up the letter as he banged around in the bathroom.

Dear Nathan and Claudie,

I'm afraid I've taken a somewhat larger cut than you planned. I'm sorry. But it happens I have an urgent need of cash. People's lives at stake, that kind of thing. I left you a smidgeon (in the bathroom under the sink),

*and of course I gave some to your lovely niece. Sorry
I said it was all from me, but I thought it best so you
wouldn't have to answer difficult questions.*

*Please forgive me. Someday I hope to make up to you.
And please, please don't come looking for me. You'd
only find yourself in a nest of snakes.*

Claudie please take care of my favorite old coot.

Love, Dani

*PS: I'm afraid I reported your passport stolen. Just to
make sure you don't do something hasty.*

Nathan came out of the bathroom with a plastic wrapped bundle. It looked about the same size as the kids'. He flung it down on the table and took the other chair.

"It's okay, Nathan. I don't really need the money. It was a nice little fantasy while it lasted. I'd probably feel guilty about profiting from what happened. Like I was a paid assassin or something. Ellie and Eric have their money for the clinic and that looks like enough for you to travel wherever you want. First class, too." She reached across the table and took his hand. He looked over to her and she was relieved that the anger started to dissipate. He put his other hand over hers and smiled.

"It was a nice fantasy, wasn't it?"

Claudie nodded. She looked around the RV and sniffed.

"We really should get this detailed. I don't fancy traveling around with the smell of beer and dope soaked into everything."

"You still want to travel with me? It'll be rather boring after this."

"Nah. You can entertain me with more philosophical turtle jokes."

"Eh? Oh, yeah, turtles all the way down."

On Monday, Claudie and Nathan left the RV at King's, who claimed to have a guy who'd make the RV like new. They took the scenic route and explored the Hells Gate area along the Rogue River. Claudie had called Hoyt about her car. It was ready to go. She found out that nearly all the marijuana had been recovered on Sunday and was now safely on its way to Portland. The State Police still didn't know who'd stolen it for certain, but Hammer Head was still the most likely person of interest. Claudie assumed the dead bodies had not been discovered yet, or identified. She'd be jumpy about this for a good long while.

She drove into Merlin and parked the Subaru at Hoyt's garage. Nathan got out and started to pull her gear out of the back of the car. Claudie and Buddy went into the office. Hoyt came in from the garage side, wiping his hands on an old red cloth. Nathan came in and Claudie handed him the key while Hoyt ran her credit card.

The bill settled, she opened the back door of the BMW and

Buddy hopped in. In the driver's seat she adjusted the mirrors and then backed the car out. The sun angled in and the glare blinded her for a second.

"Could you open the glove box? I have some sunglasses in there."

"Sure. Good Lord, what's this?" Nathan held up a blackened leather pouch.

"I found that at the campground the morning after they kidnapped you. Is it yours?"

He started laughing. Carefully he pried a flap open and extracted a blue booklet. Claudie realized it was a US passport.

"This is a miracle." He stared out the windshield, lost in thought for a bit. Nathan snorted and slapped the passport against his hands a couple of times.

"Didn't Dani say she reported your passport stolen?"

"Yes she did, clever girl. She missed one thing." He held the passport open for Claudie to glance at.

"That's not your name."

"Exactly. This was a back-up in case I ever got into trouble."

"But isn't it illegal?"

"No. This is a genuine passport, issued by our government."

"Nathan, we have a long drive home. I think it's time you told me what exactly you did for our government."

Nathan smiled at her. "I told you the truth. I did consulting work. I tracked money. Bad guys move money around all the time. If we can find it, track it, we can stop them from doing bad things with it. Of course that makes the bad guys very unhappy with the analysts who do this. I had this passport in case I ever had to run."

"Are there bad guys still after you?"

"I don't think so. It's been over five years. Most of those jokers have been eliminated. That was Dani's job."

"She's an assassin?"

"Better than that. Her motto is, 'confusion to our enemies'. As Sun Tzu would say, 'The supreme art of war is to subdue the enemy without fighting.' She liked to get them fighting each other. They're all paranoid. All she had to do was feed them bad information. I helped with that a little."

Claudie looked at the passport in his hands. "Do you think she's after more of these bad guys?"

"I thought she'd retired. Who knows?" His eyes got a far-away look in them.

Claudie reached I5 and decided that going north to Eugene and then taking the McKenzie River highway would be quicker than working their way over to Highway 97 in the east. She pulled onto the interstate and they drove in silence for a while.

They stopped in Springfield and picked up burgers to go. Nathan was still quiet and Claudie began to worry.

"It's been an hour since you've said a word, Nathan."

"What? Oh, I'm sorry."

Claudie let out an irritated sigh, "That's it? Tell me what you're thinking. I'm getting worried that you're planning something foolish."

"I was just thinking about Italy. Kay and I traveled there a lot when I was teaching."

"Isn't that where Ellie said she met Dani?"

"I believe so."

"Are you thinking about going there and looking for Dani?"

"Oh, no. She'd never go there. Too obvious. But if we went, we might meet someone there who might be able to tell me where she's gone to ground. Might even be able to tell us what she's gotten mixed up in."

"Us?"

"Well, sure. You said you'd like to travel. There's this little town in Sardinia. I'd like to show it to you. There's this incredible old castle on the hill, not a lot of tourists this time of year. What do you say?"

Suddenly, Claudie felt her life lurch. She'd looked forward to exploring a relationship with Nathan, but this was something else. It was … it was exciting.

"I'm in. When do we leave?"

About the Author

Jeanette Hubbard was brought up in Iowa to be a very good girl. Then she moved to Portland, Oregon, the city that prides itself on weird. She has utilized her degree in English from the University of Iowa in a variety of jobs, including driving a school bus, selling car insurance, and growing (and sometimes killing) plants at her wholesale nursery west of Portland. She now lives with her Border collie Buddy, Mitten the monster cat, her roommate's two demented small dogs, a miniature horse, and two chickens in a small house. Actually, the horse and chickens live in the backyard.

Chasing Nathan is her second published novel.

www.jeanettehubbard.com